WE THE CHILDREN

BENJAMIN PRATT & THE
KEEPERS OF THE SCHOOL
WE THE CHILDREN
BOOK 1

ANDREW CLEMENTS
ILLUSTRATED BY ADAM STOWER

Atheneum Books for Young Readers
New York London Toronto Sydney

ATHENEUM BOOKS FOR YOUNG READERS
An imprint of Simon & Schuster Children's Publishing Division
1230 Avenue of the Americas, New York, New York 10020
This book is a work of fiction. Any references to historical events, real people, or real locales are used fictitiously. Other names, characters, places, and incidents are products of the author's imagination, and any resemblance to actual events or locales or persons, living or dead, is entirely coincidental.
Text copyright © 2010 by Andrew Clements
Illustrations copyright © 2010 by Adam Stower
All rights reserved, including the right of reproduction in whole or in part in any form.
ATHENEUM BOOKS FOR YOUNG READERS is a registered trademark of Simon & Schuster, Inc.
For information about special discounts for bulk purchases, please contact
Simon & Schuster Special Sales at 1-866-506-1949 or business@simonandschuster.com.
The Simon & Schuster Speakers Bureau can bring authors to your live event. For more information or to book an event, contact the Simon & Schuster Speakers Bureau at 1-866-248-3049 or visit our website at www.simonspeakers.com.
Also available in an Atheneum Books for Young Readers hardcover edition
Book design by Sonia Chaghatzbanian
The text for this book is set in Veronan.
The illustrations for this book are rendered in pen and ink.
Manufactured in the United States of America
0911 MTN
First Atheneum Books for Young Readers paperback edition April 2011
10 9 8 7 6 5 4 3 2
The Library of Congress has cataloged the hardcover edition as follows:
Clements, Andrew, 1949–
We the children/Andrew Clements; illustrated by Adam Stower. —
p. cm. — (Benjamin Pratt and the keepers of the school)
Summary: Sixth-grader Ben Pratt's life is full of changes that he does not like—his parents' separation and the plan to demolish his seaside school to build an amusement park—but when the school janitor gives him a tarnished coin with some old engravings and then dies, Ben is drawn into an effort to keep the school from being destroyed.
ISBN 978-1-4169-3886-6 (hc)
[1. Mystery and detective stories. 2. Schools—Fiction. 3. Sailing—fiction.]
I. Stower, Adam, ill. II Title.
PZ7.C59118Wd2010
[Fic]—dc22   2009036428
ISBN 978-1-4169-3907-8 (pbk)

For Faynia Davis,
a friend and inspiration
—A. C.

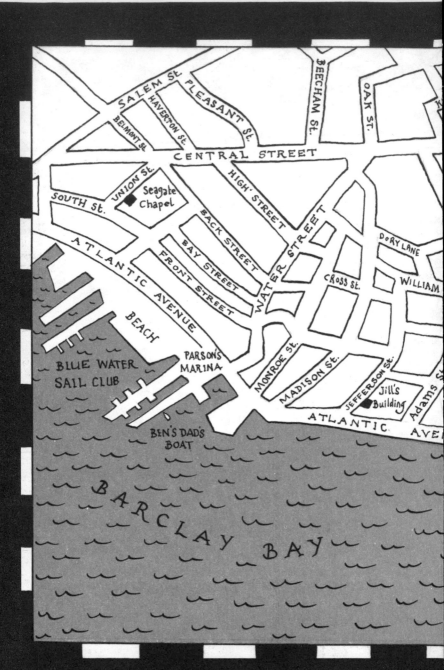

CHAPTER 1

Promise

As the ship's bell clanged through the school's hallway for the third time, Ben ran his tongue back and forth across the porcelain caps that covered his front teeth, a nervous habit. And he was nervous because he was late. Again.

When she was being the art teacher, Ms. Wilton was full of smiles and fun and two dozen clever ways to be creative with egg cartons and yarn—but in homeroom she was different. More like a drill sergeant. Or a prison guard. Still, maybe if he got to his seat before she took attendance, he *might* not have to stay after school. Again.

The art room was in the original school building, and Ben was still hurrying through the Annex, the newer part of the school. But the long connecting hallway was empty, so he put on a burst of speed. He banged through the double doors at a dead run, slowed a little for the last corner, then sprinted for the art room.

Halfway there, he stopped in his tracks.

"Mr. Keane—are you okay?"

It was a stupid question. The janitor was dragging his left leg as he used the handle of a big dust mop like a crutch, trying to get himself through the doorway into his workroom. His face was pale, twisted with pain.

"Help me . . . sit down." His breathing was ragged, his voice raspy.

Ben gulped. "I should call 9-1-1."

"Already did, and I told 'em where to find me," the man growled. "Just get me . . . to that chair."

With one arm across Ben's shoulders, Mr. Keane groaned with each step, then eased himself into a chair by the workbench.

"Sh-should I get the school nurse?"

Mr. Keane's eyes flashed, and his shock of white hair was wilder and messier than usual. "That windbag? No—I broke my ankle or somethin' on the stairs, and it hurts like the devil. And it means I'm gonna be laid up the rest of the school year. And you can stop lookin' so scared. I'm not mad at *you*, I'm just . . . *mad*."

As he snarled that last word, Ben saw his yellowed teeth. And he remembered why all the kids at Oakes School tried to steer clear of old man Keane.

A distant siren began to wail, then a second one. Edgeport wasn't a big town, so the sound got louder by the second.

From under his bushy eyebrows, Mr. Keane looked up into Ben's face. "I know you, don't I?"

Ben nodded. "You helped me and my dad scrape the hull of our sailboat two summers ago. Over at Parson's Marina." He remembered that Mr. Keane had been sharp and impatient the entire week, no fun at all.

"Right—you're the Pratt kid."

"I'm Ben . . . Benjamin."

The janitor kept looking into his face, and Ben felt like he was in a police lineup. Then the man suddenly nodded, as if he was agreeing with someone.

He straightened his injured leg, gasping in pain, pushed a hand into his front pocket, then pulled it back out.

"Stick out your hand."

Startled, Ben said, "What?"

"You hard a' hearing? *Stick out your hand!*"

Ben did, and Mr. Keane grabbed hold and pressed something into his palm, quickly closing the boy's fingers around it. Then he clamped Ben's fist inside his leathery grip. Ben wanted to yank his hand loose and run, but he wasn't sure he could break free . . . and part of him didn't want to. Even though he was frightened, he was curious, too. So he just gulped and stood there, eyes wide, staring at the faded blue anchor tattooed on the man's wrist.

"This thing in your hand? I've been carryin' it around with me every day for *forty-three years*. Tom Benton was the janitor here before me, and the day he retired, he handed it to me. And before Tom Benton, it was in Jimmy Conklin's pocket for thirty-some years, and before *that*, the other janitors had it—every one of 'em, all the way back to the very first man hired by Captain Oakes himself when he founded the school. Look at it . . . but first promise that you'll keep all this secret." He squinted up into Ben's face, his blue eyes bright and feverish. "Do you swear?"

Ben's mouth was dry. He'd have said anything to get this scary old guy with bad breath to let go of him. He whispered, "I swear."

Mr. Keane released his hand, and Ben opened his fingers.

And then he stared. It was a large gold coin with rounded edges, smooth as a beach pebble.

Outside, the sirens were closing in fast.

"See the writing? Read it."

First and always
my School belongs
to the children
DEFEND IT
Duncan Oakes
1783

With shaky hands, Ben held the coin up to catch more light. The words stamped into the soft metal had been worn away to shadows, barely visible.

He read aloud, still whispering. "'If attacked, look nor'-nor'east from amidships on the upper deck.'" He turned the coin over. "'First and always, my school belongs to the children. DEFEND IT. Duncan Oakes, 1783.'"

Mr. Keane's eyes flashed. "You know about the town council, right? How they sold this school and all the land? And how they're tearin' the place down in June? If that's not an *attack*, then I don't know what is."

He stopped talking and sat still. He seemed to soften, and when he spoke, for a moment he sounded almost childlike. "I know I'm just the guy who cleans up and all, but I love it here, with the wind comin' in off the water, and bein' able to see halfway to England. And all the kids love it too—best piece of coast for thirty miles, north or south. And this place? This is a *school*, and Captain Oakes meant it to stay that way, come blood or blue thunder. And I am *not* giving it up without a fight. And I am *not* giving this coin to that new janitor—I told him too much already." His

6

face darkened, and he spat the man's name into the air. "*Lyman*—you know who he is?"

Ben nodded. The assistant custodian was hard to miss, very tall and thin. He had been working at the school since right after winter vacation.

"Lyman's a *snake*. Him, the principal, the superintendent—don't trust any of 'em, you hear?"

The principal? Ben thought. And the superintendent? What do they have to do with any of this?

The sirens stopped, and Ben heard banging doors, then commotion and shouting in the hallway leading from the Annex.

The janitor's breathing was forced, and his face had gone chalky white. But he grabbed Ben's wrist with surprising strength and pushed out one more sentence. "Captain Oakes said this school *belongs* to the kids. So that coin is yours now, and the fight is yours too—*yours!*"

The hairs on Ben's neck stood up. Fight? What fight? This is crazy!

Two paramedics burst into the room, a woman and a man, both wearing bright green gloves. A policeman and Mrs. Hendon, the school secretary, stood out in the hallway.

"Move!" the woman barked. "We're getting him out of here!"

Mr. Keane let go of Ben's wrist, and Ben jumped to one side, his heart pounding, the coin hidden in his hand.

The woman gave the janitor a quick exam, then nodded at her partner and said, "He's good to go—just watch the left leg."

And as they lifted the custodian onto the gurney and then strapped him down flat, the old man's eyes never left Ben's face.

As they wheeled him out, Mrs. Hendon came into the workroom and said, "I'm glad you were here to help him, Ben. Are you all right?"

"Sure, I'm fine."

"Well, you'd better get along to class now."

Ben picked up his backpack and headed toward the art room. And just before he opened the door, both sirens began wailing again.

CHAPTER 2

Moments of Silence

"So, what do you know about Duncan Oakes?"

Jill Acton stared across the lunch table at Ben and stopped chewing the bite of tuna salad sandwich she had just stuffed into her mouth.

"Hwuh?"

"Captain Oakes," Ben said. "What do you know about him?"

Jill took a glug of milk, wiped her mouth on the sleeve of her shirt, and said, "I know he's a weirdo—a *dead* weirdo. And he was rich. And he probably enjoyed making small children miserable, or else he wouldn't have turned his big old building into a school—it should have been a prison. Or a pet hospital. Anything but a school. Okay, that's too harsh. I guess I'm just ready for a long break. Like a whole summer."

"You really think Oakes was weird?" asked Ben.

"What—you *don't*?" said Jill. "Who has himself *buried* in the middle of a school playground? And who designs his own giant tombstone so it has a place for a *seesaw*? And then sticks iron rings everywhere so kids can climb all over it? I'll tell you who: one seriously *weird* old lunatic."

Ben nodded thoughtfully as he finished his second piece of chocolate cake. The sixth graders ate lunch first, so there was always plenty of cake, and Ben loved cake. And he usually ate dessert first.

Jill had a good point about the captain's tombstone. It was a massive dome of gray granite, about eight feet across and almost five feet tall—except where it was notched for a seesaw. The seesaw board had been removed years ago for safety reasons, but the gravestone was smack in the middle of the playground at the Captain Duncan Oakes School, and kids still scrambled all over it every day during recess. It was definitely an odd spot for a man to have himself buried. And that life-sized portrait of the captain up on the third-floor hallway? This was a man who did not want to be forgotten.

Jill narrowed her eyes, took another huge bite of sandwich, and mumbled, "Hacomyowrinressedncapnoakesalvasudn?"

Ben didn't want to discuss that, so he shrugged and took his own huge bite of grilled cheese.

Truth was, he had been thinking about Captain Oakes the whole morning. And about the gold coin. And the writing on it. And about everything the janitor had said to him.

Was he supposed to be doing something about this stuff? Like getting Mr. Keane's phone number, or maybe going over to his house to talk some more? Because he had tons of questions. It was all just so . . . *weird.* Jill had picked the right word.

He glanced her way, and the tuna sandwich was gone. Now she was destroying half a dozen carrot sticks. Ben was sure the guys he usually ate with had spotted him, sitting here with her. They had to be wondering why. Couldn't be helped. Right now he needed some real brainpower—and she was smarter than all of them put together.

While Ben was still chewing, the intercom speaker

on the wall of the cafeteria crackled, followed by one clang from the ship's bell.

"I need everyone's attention for an important announcement."

It was the principal, Mr. Telmer, and the cafeteria quieted down a notch or two.

"For many years Mr. Roger Keane has been head custodian here at Captain Oakes School. His wife just called me to say that he was taken to the hospital this morning with what seemed like a simple problem, but it became more serious. And I'm sad to tell you that about an hour ago, Mr. Keane passed away. He was a good man and a hard worker, and I know all of us will miss him. So let's please take a few moments of silence together now while we remember Mr. Keane."

The lunchroom went completely still except for the humming of the milk cooler.

Ben felt like the cafeteria was spinning. He could barely breathe. Dead? He was *dead*? They had talked—just a few hours ago. And now . . . he was dead.

After about twenty seconds, the principal said, "Thank you, and I want everyone to have a safe afternoon."

As the cafeteria came back to life, Jill narrowed her eyes at Ben. "You look like you're gonna be sick. Are you okay?"

Ben nodded and tried to smile. Then he took a drink of milk, but it tasted bitter. He felt dizzy.

"Are you okay?" Jill asked again.

"I'm fine," he said.

But it wasn't true.

Ben got up to go dump his tray, and in the front pocket of his cargo pants he felt an unfamiliar weight banging against his leg—the gold coin.

And as he headed out for recess, there was the new janitor, tall and thin, standing beside the playground door. He was leaning on the handle of a big dust mop—probably the same mop Mr. Keane had used this morning. As a crutch. Before he died.

Ben and the janitor made eye contact, and Lyman nodded slightly, his long face expressionless. Then he reached out with his foot and pushed the door open.

"Thanks," said Ben, and went outside, forcing himself not to run his tongue across his front teeth.

A brisk onshore breeze was blowing, and he pulled in deep breaths of cool, salty air. He was one of the first kids on the playground, and he walked

straight for the big rock with the name OAKES cut deep into the stone, each letter eight inches tall.

Grabbing one of the iron rings, he put the toes of a sneaker into the flat groove made by the bottom of the *E*, pulled himself up, and clambered to the top. The granite was warm from the May sunshine.

Ben looked past the south corner of the old brick building, through the oak and maple and beech trees, across the school's front lawn to the harbor wall. And then his eyes reached all the way out across the blue waves of the bay. A wide-open view like this usually calmed him down, helped him think clearly. Today it wasn't working, and Ben knew why. He'd probably been the last person at school to talk to the old guy. Before he died. And the man had been so serious about everything, and so . . . trusting. And how had Ben responded to him? Fear. Plus a little disgust. He'd almost been glad to see the paramedics haul him away.

That talk with the janitor hadn't been some ordinary little chat. Ben had looked into the man's eyes while he swore to keep a secret. Then he had accepted a token, a gold coin. From a dead man.

And on that coin, there was a direct command from Captain Oakes—another dead man.

Then there had been talk of the attack on the school. And talk about fighting to defend the place.

He could still feel Mr. Keane's grip on his wrist.

During the past eleven and a half years, nothing had prepared Ben for something like this. So he tapped his tongue against his capped front teeth and kept looking out to sea.

He heard someone climbing the rock from behind, and a few seconds later Jill sat beside him.

She was quiet for a minute, then said, "Is this about your parents?"

Ben shook his head. "Nope." No way did he want to think about *that*, not today.

His mom and dad were going through some problems, and Jill was the only other kid at school who knew about it. Ben sort of wished he hadn't told her. He understood that she wanted to help, but if he ever got the least bit quiet or thoughtful, she always assumed he was worried about his parents' separation.

And he *was* worried about it. But not constantly.

"So what's bugging you?" she said. "Is this about old man Keane? I mean, I'm sorry when anybody kicks the bucket—it's a lousy thing. But sad stuff happens all the time, so why stress out about it? That's what I say."

Ben had to smile a little at the way she put it. "Yeah, I guess that makes sense."

After a few seconds, Jill said, "So . . . this must be something else then—I know. You're all *scared* about the big social studies test this afternoon, right?"

That made them both laugh, because Ben was a total brain in that class.

He jumped down off the gravestone and looked up at her. "Listen, I'm fine. Really. But thanks for asking. And now I'm going to the library to review some more for that big test . . . because I'm so scared about it. Later."

Walking away, Ben felt a little better, and he was glad Jill had come looking for him. But he needed more time alone. He had a lot to think about.

CHAPTER 3

Attack

Fifth period still had ten minutes to go, and Ben was the first to finish the test, which happened a lot in social studies. Kings and queens, generals and presidents, wars and battles and maps and time lines—he loved seeing how all the people and events fit together. It was like a huge jigsaw puzzle.

He turned the test over, folded his arms on top of it, and put his head down. He tried to let his mind go blank, tried to let all the tangled events of the day drift away.

But as he stared at the far wall, the portrait of George Washington caught his attention. And then he saw that the man had blue eyes. And that made him start thinking about Mr. Keane again. And he didn't want to.

So he closed his eyes. Then he yawned and started feeling like he might fall asleep. And he didn't want to do that, either.

So he made himself sit up, and he turned his head to look out the window awhile.

As always, the view was fantastic—even better than the view from the captain's tombstone. Mrs. Hinman's room was on the third floor of the original Oakes School, and the big windows faced due east. Because the building was exactly fifty feet from the water's edge, Ben could see three distant sailboats and a fishing trawler cutting across Barclay Bay. Seagulls hovered above the shoreline, wings almost motionless, beaks aimed downward as they scanned for food. And a few hundred yards out, two kayakers made their way south, paddles flashing in the sunlight, both boats bright yellow against the blue waves.

This building had been a school since 1783, and Ben thought of all the other kids like him— thousands and thousands of them—who had sat staring out to sea through these very same windows, wishing they were onboard some ship, sailing away from Massachusetts, headed for distant lands.

Ben had lived all his life a few blocks from this place. His mom and dad had pushed him on the playground swings back when he was little. Ben had climbed most of the trees and had played twilight games of kick-the-can on the wide lawns. He had spent hot afternoons sitting on the harborside wall with a fishing pole.

And in just four weeks, the old school would be completely gone, torn down and hauled away.

Because it was like Mr. Keane had said: The Edgeport Town Council had voted, and the school and the twenty acres around it had been sold to a big company that wanted to build a theme park. But the sale hadn't happened overnight or anything. For the past several years it seemed like every time he flipped past the local cable TV channel, there was some noisy public hearing about it. And Ben knew he had mostly tuned it all out. Because why try to fight against the inevitable? The town council had called the final deal a great step forward, "a leap of progress for Edgeport." But to Ben it looked like the past had done battle with the future, and, as usual, the future had won. The whole town was changing faster and faster, and Ben hated it.

As he stared out to sea, a sarcastic smile formed on his lips, almost a sneer. *Welcome to the exciting new theme of Benjamin Pratt's life—change.*

When his parents separated two months ago, it had come as a complete surprise. One morning it was, "Ben, your mom and I have something we all need to discuss," and the next day his dad had moved out.

His dad still lived close by—actually, very close. He was staying on their sailboat, which was docked at Parson's Marina, less than half a mile south of the school along the waterfront. So he got to see his dad all the time.

But the separation was a huge, unwelcome change.

A sudden motion in the air off to the right caught Ben's eye. It wasn't a gull or some other seabird out there. No, this thing was big—as big as a mailbox on a street corner, except it was reddish brown, and wider at the bottom than it was at the top. The thing was gliding away in a low, lazy arc out over the water of the bay. But then it slowed until it hung in midair about three hundred feet away from the old school building.

That's strange.

And as he watched, this odd-shaped lump began moving again, heading straight back toward the school, picking up speed, coming faster and faster.

Ben tried to shout a warning, tried to scream, *Hey! That thing! It's coming, it's almost here!* But fear clamped his throat shut.

He blinked his eyes wider as the thing neared, and when it was just feet away from the windows of his third-floor classroom, he suddenly knew what it was—a wrecking ball, three tons of scarred, rusty steel, hissing through the salty air at forty miles an hour.

It hit the building like a locomotive, splintering the glass and wood of the window frames. Bricks and chunks of granite from the outer wall flew past Ben's head, shattering the slate blackboards. The rounded blob of metal tore upward through the old wooden

floorboards, breaching like an angry whale, rising toward the ceiling. Electric wires snapped and sparked and crackled through a fog of plaster dust. Desks and chairs, books and computers, maps and papers flew upward and seemed to hang in midair. Kids screamed and rushed for the door, only to see that door smashed to bits.

And Ben still couldn't move, couldn't make a sound.

Finally he found his voice and shouted, "Stop! Stop it! Stop it *now*!"

A distant engine growled, and then came a squealing sound. The thick cable at the top of the wrecking ball snapped taut, and the thing slithered away through the huge hole it had ripped in the front of the school.

But the ball swung out over the harbor, and then started to rush back toward the building.

Ben screamed again, "No! *No!*"

"Ben!"

Someone grabbed him by the shoulder, tried to pull him to safety as the ball rushed closer.

"Ben!"

"No!" he yelled, and he tried to pull the hand off his shoulder.

He turned—and saw his father.

Terrified, he yelled, "Dad! You've got to get out of here!"

"Come on, Ben, wake up. Wake all the way up."

Ben sat up straight and looked around, his eyes wild, his brown hair stuck to his forehead. It was Mrs. Hinman who'd been shaking him, and all the kids in the class stared, a few looking concerned, but most of them laughing and whispering to one another.

Mrs. Hinman clapped her hands twice. "Hush, everyone—quiet. You've got five more minutes to finish the test." The room went silent again.

Ben heard a snort from his right, and turned to see Robert Gerritt with a big grin on his face—which was just like him. He loved it whenever Ben messed up.

Mrs. Hinman could see Ben was all right, so she walked back to the front of the class.

And Ben was all right, sort of.

He sat there, his face bright red, his palms pressed flat against the test papers on his desk. His heart was still pounding, partly from embarrassment, but mostly because that dream had been so awful.

He turned to sneak a quick peek out the windows, just to be sure things really were okay.

No wrecking ball, not today.

But like his mom's and dad's separation, that part wasn't a dream. The wrecking ball was coming for real. And soon.

Because Mr. Keane was right: The school was definitely under attack.

CHAPTER 4

Whiff

Ben knew that Ms. Wilton would have excused his tardiness for homeroom if he had explained about stopping to help Mr. Keane. But he didn't want to talk to anybody about that, especially now that the man was dead. And he also hoped the school secretary didn't tell anyone he was there in the workroom. Because back when he was in first grade, a kindergarten teacher had died in a car crash, and someone had made him spend half an hour with a grief counselor. And he didn't want to have to do that again. Ever.

So Ben walked into the art room exactly five minutes after the dismissal bell—because being late for detention meant staying *two* days after school.

He set his book bag on a table near the back of the room. Ms. Wilton was standing at the big paint-spattered sink in the front corner, a bucket in one hand and a large sponge in the other. There was a puddle of water around her feet. When she heard him pull out his chair, she jerked her head around.

"Oh, good, it's you. Go get the janitor and tell him I've got a flood here—the drain is clogged and the faucet is broken. Hurry!"

Ben ducked back into the hallway and trotted toward the front of the building. In less than thirty seconds he was at the door of the custodian's workroom—for the second time today. He didn't want to be anywhere near that place, but he had no choice, so he knocked.

Nothing.

He knocked a second time, then called, "Mr. Lyman?"

From far down the hall, a deep voice boomed out, "Somebody looking for me?"

Ben jogged all the way to the front hall, and when he turned the corner, the custodian was coming out of the nurse's office. He was pushing a wheeled metal bucket with a mop handle sticking up out of the yellow wringer. The sharp smell of vomit brought Ben to a sudden stop.

"Ms. Wilton sent me from the art room. She says there's a broken faucet and a clogged sink. It's leaking on the floor."

Mr. Lyman, his dark brown eyes set deep in his skull, scowled and looked down at Ben. "Third time since February," he said, and began pushing the bucket forward again.

As they headed toward the rear of the building, the janitor's longer stride put him out ahead right away, and Ben didn't try to keep up. He hated that smell, plus he was in no great rush to get back to detention.

So he took a long drink at the water fountain, then dawdled along and looked at a big bulletin board about dinosaurs.

When he came to the custodian's room again, he tiptoed to the doorway and looked in. Lyman was in front of the workbench, rummaging through some metal bins and muttering to himself.

To the right of the bench Ben saw a red door with the words BOILER ROOM painted in black letters, and in yellow and black letters above the doorknob, a warning: CAUTION: STEPS DOWN.

A basement? That seemed odd for a building this close to the water. But he quickly forgot about that as his eye drifted along to the next wall.

Several sheets of thick plastic had been joined together to make a protective cover, and behind it there was an assortment of tools—block planes, squares and rules, handsaws, augers and braces, chisels, spokeshaves, several hatchets, wooden mallets, iron pliers and wrenches, and at least a dozen hammers of all sorts and shapes and sizes. There were close to a hundred different tools, all looking well used, but each in excellent condition. And they were old—very, very old. He and his dad both loved old tools, so Ben pulled out his cell phone, activated the camera, and took three overlapping pictures. What a collection!

Without turning, Lyman suddenly said, "Want to make yourself useful?"

Ben jumped a little. "Um . . . okay."

"Dump the bucket into the sink there and then rinse out the mop. Think you can handle that?" There was a challenge in his voice.

"Sure," said Ben, and he rolled the bucket over to the wide porcelain sink.

He was big for his age and plenty strong, so lifting the bucket wasn't a problem. The problem was the smell—he almost gagged as he dumped the filthy water. Little bits that looked like orange cottage cheese swirled around and around before disappearing down the drain.

He turned on a blast of hot water, which made a cloud of foul steam rise up around him. Ben fought back another urge to throw up, and stepped away. He sucked in a deep breath and held it as he moved forward and quickly rinsed out the bucket and set it on the floor. Then he picked up the mop by its long handle and stuck the tangled mass of cotton strings into the hot water.

He exhaled loudly, then took another cautious breath . . . Gross! The smell was everywhere. He turned from the sink to see Lyman watching him.

"Pretty sure it was you I saw this morning—leaving the room here. After they hauled the old man away."

Startled, Ben quickly turned back to the sink and grabbed the mop handle, holding the strings under the water. His heart began thumping, and he felt his face start to heat up. But he pretended to be busy with the cleanup.

When he glanced over at the bench again, the janitor was dropping nuts and bolts and washers into a small plastic bag. As if he knew Ben was watching, he began talking again.

"Strange bird, that one. But he sure knew this building. Loved the place. Hated how it's gonna get torn down. And he was half crazy, too—said he had a way to stop it. Said he took *his* orders straight from Captain Oakes himself." Lyman paused. "You two probably talked a little, eh? Or maybe he gave you something?"

Ben squeezed the mop handle so hard that his knuckles went white. Did Lyman know about the coin? Had Mr. Keane told him about it . . . or maybe even shown it to him? He took a quick breath, and this time the sharp smell hit him like a kick in the stomach.

He lunged forward and bent over the big bucket, grabbing it with both hands. He didn't quite throw up, but he did get a taste of that second piece of chocolate cake from lunch.

Ben backed away from the sink again, gasping for air, furious at himself for seeming so weak. Still, he was glad to have an excuse for not talking. Because he wasn't going to tell Lyman a thing. Ever. He had sworn not to.

Lyman smiled. "Throw a cup of that powder from the white pail onto the mop head—helps cut the stink. And do the same for the bucket."

Ben did as he was told, but he didn't like the look of the man's smile. Lyman wasn't just fishing for information. He was also having a little fun. The guy thought he was being clever, getting some dumb kid to do a nasty job for him.

And Ben remembered the old janitor's warning: *Lyman's a snake!*

As the custodian began tossing tools into a canvas bag, he said, "How about you roll that bucket and mop over to the art room for me? I'll be along in a minute."

"No thanks," said Ben. "I'm going to go wash my hands."

Turning around to face him, Lyman frowned. "You can wash up right there at the sink. And then push that bucket for me."

Ben looked him in the eye and shook his head. Speaking politely, he said, "Thanks, but I'd rather not." Then he turned around and walked out.

He wanted to shout, *You are* not *my boss, and I will tell you* nothing*!* But shouting hadn't been necessary. The message got through anyway, loud and clear.

And politely.

When Ben slipped into the back of the art room five minutes later, his hands were very clean. He sat at the table, opened his book bag, and took out some index cards and a biography of Lincoln. But he couldn't really read—too much to think about. So he mostly sketched and doodled on the index cards.

Ms. Wilton was bustling around, hanging artwork and preparing materials for the next day. She kept trying to make small talk with Lyman, but he was busy, bent over the sink up front. He replied with an occasional nod or grunt.

Ben glanced up from his doodling now and then—carefully. He didn't want any eye contact, but the way the janitor had acted in the workroom made him curious, especially since Mr. Keane had warned him about Lyman. And the repair work was interesting, too. He had helped his dad do a lot of fix-up projects on their old house—the house where his mom lived now. And on the boat, too.

As he made little drawings and designs, a fragment of Mr. Keane's warning about Lyman popped into Ben's mind: I told him too much already. So maybe *that* was why he had asked all those questions back in the workroom.

Watching him at the art room sink, Ben quickly saw that this man was a good mechanic. After shutting off the water supply, Lyman used a long, springy wire to unclog the drain. Then he replaced the worn-out washers and turned the water back on. He tested the faucets and the drain, and finally he mopped the floor. The whole job only took him about ten minutes.

Done, the custodian gathered up his tools. As he walked toward the back tables on his way out the door, Ben kept his eyes glued to his book, and he put his hand over a little sketch he had made on an index card—a tall man with a long, thin face. And he tried to keep his tongue still. But he could feel Lyman looking at him, evaluating him.

And as the wheeled bucket rolled past and out into the hallway, Ben caught another faint whiff of vomit.

CHAPTER 5

Trust

It was almost three thirty, and Ben glanced back over his shoulder as he went down the front steps of the school. He had made it from the art room, up to his locker on the third floor, and then back down to the front doors, all without running into the janitor—or smelling any more vomit. A clean getaway.

Outside in the bright sun and clear ocean breeze, he wanted to laugh at himself for feeling so spooked by Lyman.

But he didn't laugh, didn't even smile. The man was . . . *reptilian*—a word he had noticed on that dinosaur bulletin board.

He hurried straight ahead to the seawall, and

then turned right and went south, still on the school grounds. One . . . two . . . three . . . As he walked, Ben began to count the bollards, squat little stumps of iron dotted along the harbor wall. Sailors had once used them for tying ships to the shore, but now they were mostly seagull perches.

Except at this moment, he spotted Jill sitting on one about thirty feet away, face tipped toward the sun, her straight brown hair tucked behind one ear and slanted across her neck. And Ben decided that when her mouth wasn't full of tuna salad, she was sort of pretty.

"Hey," Ben called. "What are you doing here?" But he knew exactly what she was doing.

She turned and smiled. "Just hanging out—nice weather."

When he got closer, she picked up her back-pack and walked alongside him. They left the school grounds, crossed Washington Street, and continued south on the harbor walk beside Atlantic Avenue, neither of them talking.

About fifty yards out on the water to their left, someone suddenly yelled, "Jibe-ho!"

They both turned just in time to see a tall white

sail go whipping from one side to the other of a low-slung boat—while the two people on board ducked low to keep from being whacked by it. Ten seconds later, the guy steering the sailboat shouted the command again—"Jibe-ho!"—and again, both of them ducked as the sail went flying past the other way, just inches above their heads.

Jill shook her head. "Look at those guys—they've been out there almost every afternoon for the past two weeks, yelling stuff like 'starboard,' and 'jive-ho'—they sound like Captain Hook or something."

Jill walked home this way every day, unless she had after-school orchestra and needed a ride for her cello. She and her parents and her two little brothers lived in a condo on Jefferson Street.

"Yeah," she went on, "and they probably walk around with eye patches, and carry parrots on their shoulders—'Avast there, matey!' And that spray shooting up all over the place? They've got to be freezing out there. Why would anyone want to *do* that?"

"First of all," Ben said, "it's not *jive*-ho,' it's *jibe*-ho'—'jibe,' with a *b*. And second, that's a warning you have to yell when you steer off the wind like that, or else someone'll get killed when the sail whips past your head. And those guys definitely know what they are doing. That's Tom Arndt and Ray Cahill, two of the top racers on the East Coast, and they're training for the U.S. Junior Championships in August. And I'll bet you anything they've got wet suits on under their foul-weather gear, so they're warm as toast. And . . . I wish *I* was out there, right now."

Jill stared at him. "So . . . like, what? You're a *sailor?*"

Ben blushed a little. "Yup, at the Bluewater Sailing Club. I've got my first race of the season on Saturday afternoon. So it'll be my turn to freeze. And yell stuff that sounds like Captain Hook."

"On a boat like that?" she said, nodding toward the bay.

Ben shook his head. "That's a 420—that takes two people to sail it. I'm racing a boat called an Optimist. It's tiny, only about seven feet long, so you do everything yourself—man the tiller, haul the sheet, bail out the bilge, everything. But there's no jib to trim, so it's pretty basic. And its got a deeper hull, so there's not as much spray hitting you. Sometimes."

"Listen to yourself," she said, "'haul the sheet,'

'man the tiller'—it's a foreign language. And what the heck is a jib?"

Ben pointed at the 420, now tacking along parallel to the shore. "See the smaller sail there at the bow of the boat? That's the jib. And the tiller controls the blade in the water behind the boat that steers it, and the sheet is the rope that controls the mainsail. You have to learn the terms, but that's true for anything when you're new at it—even playing chess."

"So, how long have you been doing this?"

"Taking lessons? Two years. There's tons to learn, especially about racing—all these rules. But you should try it out sometime, just sailing around a little. I bet you'd like it."

"Well, maybe in August," she said. "On a calm day. When the water's not like ice."

They started walking again. Ben was headed for Parson's Marina, which was five blocks south of Jill's street. He was staying with his dad this week, because that was the deal: a week with Dad, a week with Mom.

Staying with Dad meant coming home after school to an empty sailboat, an old thirty-four-foot yawl named *Tempus Fugit*—Latin for "Time Flies."

He'd been trying to act cheerful about the new arrangements, but he hated the whole thing. He hated keeping clothes at two different places, and he hated having to remember where he was when he woke up each morning. And most of all he hated how his mom and dad avoided talking about stuff they all used to do together.

In summers past they had sailed northward along the coast as far as Nova Scotia, and one year they went south all the way to Chesapeake Bay. As a family. Mom and Dad and Ben—that's how it had always been. And that's what he wanted.

And the big plan for this summer had been a long voyage to the Bahamas, maybe even to South America. As a family.

But it wasn't happening.

The one good thing about living with his dad was the hour or two he got alone on the boat after school. His dad taught math at Beecham High School, which was about fifteen miles west. He also coached boys lacrosse, so in the spring he almost never got home before five. Which was good. Ben liked having time to think. And he also liked taking his time as he walked along the harborside. Alone.

Still, Ben was glad Jill had waited. He'd done some more thinking during detention, after Lyman left the art room. And he had made a decision.

As they passed Adams Street he said, "At lunch today? There was stuff I wasn't sure I could talk about, and then I got all freaked out after . . . well, here." He pulled the gold coin from his pocket and handed it to her. "Take a look at this."

They stopped as Jill examined the coin. She read both sides, then looked at Ben, her eyes wide. "Where did you get this?"

Ben told her everything—about helping Mr. Keane in the morning, what he'd said about the school, and his warnings about the new janitor. "And right at the end he said *I* had to fight for the school now. And he made me swear to keep it all a secret. So that's why I pretty much lost it when we heard that announcement."

Ben also described what had happened with Lyman after school. When he was done, Jill was quiet, thinking. They began walking again.

She smiled a little as she handed the coin back. "So . . . how come you decided it was okay to tell me about it?"

Ben felt a blush begin to creep up his neck, but he squashed it like a cockroach. In a cold, logical tone of voice, he said, "Because if *you* had been the kid who helped Mr. Keane this morning, he would have looked into your face instead of mine. And he would have handed the coin to you—I'm sure of it. He would have trusted you."

More silent walking. Then Jill said, "I mean, the coin is amazing and everything, and Mr. Keane probably meant all that stuff he said, like about fighting off the big attack on the school. But the whole town is serious about this thing now. And the new middle school on the other side of town? It's halfway built. And it's actually very cool—the gym is *huge*, and so's the swimming pool, and it's got a stage big enough for a whole orchestra, and the—"

"Are you *nuts*?" Ben wheeled to face her. "Remember the fifth-grade field trip to Plimouth Plantationland last year? *That* place is run by the same company that bought the school. There were probably four thousand people there the day we went, and school wasn't even out yet. And everybody had to pay *seventy dollars* just to get through the gates, not to mention all the stuff they sell inside the park. A big park like that makes millions and millions every month—*so* much money. Think what it would mean if something like that was here, right *here*. And all those dumb historical exhibits, and the cheesy rides, and . . ."

"Yeah," said Jill, "like that Giant Bucket Drop? Amy and I, we screamed *sooo* loud! And we dropped down the well six times!"

Ben talked over her. ". . . and don't forget all the cars and buses coming to town every morning, and then leaving every night. So that's pollution. And think how crowded it would be downtown, and on the beaches, and here along the harbor walk. 'Cause all those people are going to want food and souvenirs and everything. And didn't you see those posters they put up everywhere last fall? 'Coming to Edgeport: Tall Ships Ahoy! The Greatest Nautical Theme Park in the World!' They're gonna wreck the waterfront and take over the whole harbor!"

Jill cocked her head to one side. "Just last summer I heard you say it might be fun to have an amusement park in town. And you also said—"

"But that was, like, ages ago," he interrupted.

"Can't you see? They're gonna *ruin* this entire town! Not to mention the school."

"Hey," Jill snapped, "don't yell at *me*—I get what you're saying. But lots of people *want* all those new tourists. And they want the new school, too. That company is bringing *tons* of money to this town. I mean, my mom's in the Historical Society, and they've been trying to fight this for two years—they went to all the meetings, hired a big lawyer, did everything they could. And my mom says now it's all over."

Ben glared at her. "So I should go stick this coin in a drawer with my socks and forget all this. Is that it?"

Jill glared back. "No, that's *not* it, but you know what? You go and do whatever you want. 'Cause you really don't want to talk about things, or even think—you just want to shout and gripe and feel all sorry for yourself—'Boo-hoo, they're changing my happy little town!' Change *happens*, Benjamin. So face it. And go face it by yourself, because *I* don't need the drama!"

She turned on her heel and walked away.

Ben didn't try to stop her. He jammed his hands

into his front pockets and marched ahead toward the marina, a deep scowl on his face.

From the corner of his eye he saw Jill turn right onto Jefferson Street and walk uphill toward the front door of her building. And at the last possible moment, when he could have called out to her, he didn't.

He gritted his teeth, scowled harder, and walked straight ahead—with the captain's gold coin clenched in his fist.

CHAPTER 6

Tipping Point

When Ben got to the entrance of Parson's Marina, he didn't wave to Kevin, the watchman in the gatehouse. He stomped down the slanted wooden walkway, stomped along the connector pier, then headed out onto the farthest dock, still stomping, hands still jammed tight into his pockets.

The incoming tide and a light swell in the harbor made the floating dock system sway and roll underfoot. Ben didn't notice. He had spent so much time on and around boats that he never lost his balance, never got seasick.

The *Tempus Fugit* lay in its slip about halfway out the long dock, but Ben didn't stop when he reached the sailboat. He dumped his book bag onto the walkway and kept stomping.

At the very end of the dock, almost four hundred feet from shore, he stopped. He pulled the coin from his pocket and cocked his arm way back. Six noisy seagulls instantly swooped into the air in front of him, fighting for the best position in case he pitched some food. He brought his arm forward, snapped his wrist—and held tight to the coin.

He couldn't let go.

The seagulls clearly felt tricked. They gave him a good scolding, then veered off to chase a fishing boat.

Shoulders slumped, almost in tears, Ben looked toward the shoreline of the town. Instantly, his eye picked out the Oakes School with its twin chimneys and center cupola. It was the largest building along the waterfront, and the afternoon sun glinted from the weathervane. It was the major landmark, the one unmistakable feature of the town's skyline.

He thought of all the times he had sailed out of this harbor with his mom and dad. And whether a voyage was long or short, there had always been a moment when the boat would come about and head back toward Edgeport. And clearing Elder Point from the north or rounding Cape Lee from the south, when Ben saw that familiar shoreline, it had always looked like home.

He had to admit that Jill's questions had been fair. Yes, he'd known about the theme park idea for almost two years now, and yes, swapping an old school for a big amusement park used to seem like a great idea. But he was allowed to change his mind, wasn't he? Especially after what Mr. Keane said. But maybe Jill was right. Maybe he was just scared about change—any kind of change.

Focusing on the shore again, Ben tried to picture the skyline without the school. He tried to picture a big theme park there, tried to hear the screams of people on a roller coaster, tried to imagine the bright lights at night, with the constant music from the rides and the pavilions. And it made his stomach churn. It made him angry. But was he just being selfish, trying to keep everybody from changing "his happy little town"? Yeah, probably. But he had other reasons too, good ones.

The dock rose up quickly beneath his feet, then dipped low as the wake of the fishing boat rolled by. Ben flicked his tongue across his teeth, and standing there, a sudden sharp memory flooded his mind.

It was the Fourth of July when he was eight years old. He and his mom and dad had driven to Maine to visit his grandparents at their summer cottage on Shorey Pond. It was a hot day and he was wearing shorts, so the second they got out of the car, he had streaked for the water.

He dove off the end of the dock and swam toward a buoy that warned the motorboats away from the beach. As he reached the buoy, he grabbed hold of it to catch his breath. It was made of hard plastic, half red and half white, about the size of a football.

He held on and treaded water, and he wondered if he could pull the buoy completely under. In no time at all, he had wrestled it below the surface of the pond. Then he wondered what would happen if he sat on it. He pushed the buoy down deeper until he had it clamped between his knees. There he sat, and it lifted him halfway up out of the water.

He yelled, "Hey, Grampa, look at me!" and he waved his arms.

As he waved, his knees lost their grip on the slippery plastic, and at that exact moment, he looked down. The buoy shot upward and hit him squarely on the mouth.

There was yelling and screaming, and Ben's grandmother surprised everyone with her life-guarding skills. Blood gushed from Ben's upper lip, which meant a trip to the emergency room.

He sat beside his mom in the backseat. Up front, his dad gripped the steering wheel and drove their little hybrid car a lot faster than it wanted to go. His mom hugged Ben with one arm and used her free hand to help hold a towel and a plastic bag of ice against his lip.

It was a thirty-mile trip, and about halfway there, Ben suddenly pushed the ice bag away and sat up straight. He leaned forward, grabbed the rearview mirror, and tilted it until he could see his face. Then he pushed up his top lip. That made the cut hurt like crazy, but he had to look at what he could feel with his tongue: Both his front teeth were half gone, snapped clean off.

As he stared at those stubs, one a little shorter than the other, a scene poured through his mind, almost like watching a movie. He pictured the buoy shooting upward, saw it hit his mouth, and then, a second later, he saw two tiny white rectangles, his own front teeth—his *permanent* teeth—gliding slowly down and down and down through the dark water until they finally settled on the bottom of the pond.

And at that moment, he realized those white bits were still there, lying among the leaves and pine needles and rocks and tree branches and fish bones and mussel shells, down there with all the other stuff that had piled up on the bottom of Shorey Pond ever since the prehistoric glaciers melted.

Looking at his broken teeth in the mirror, he recalled seeing the teeth of an Egyptian mummy at an exhibit in Boston—a four-thousand-year-old grin. Those teeth had never been wrapped up or embalmed, because teeth last and last, all by themselves.

And sitting back down next to his mom in that speeding car, Ben knew that his very own front teeth were now part of something else. Two actual little pieces of *himself* were going to be down on the bottom of that pond. Forever.

That was the moment when Ben first glimpsed how every single moment happens only once during a person's lifetime; and how each moment arrives in a particular order, one event after another; and how every separate event shapes all the other events that come next. Forever.

And Ben also knew that from then on, his smile would be different too. *Forever.*

That Independence Day had been a tipping point in his life.

And standing on a dock more than three years later, Ben felt his life tipping again.

An old janitor had given him a special assignment, a task written in worn letters on a gold coin, a school project involving the school itself: DEFEND IT.

Throwing the coin into the sea wouldn't change the captain's command. Nothing could change it, just like nothing could ever bring back his broken teeth. Or bring Mr. Keane back. He was gone too. Forever.

And looking across the water at the school, Ben issued a command of his own, this time to himself. Because if there was some way he could save that place, he had to find it. He *had* to.

CHAPTER 7

A We Thing

When Ben got back to the *Tempus Fugit*, the cell phone in his book bag was buzzing. He glanced at his watch, yanked at the bag's zipper, and grabbed his phone. "Hi, Mom," he said. Because it was four o'clock, and his mom called him at four every single afternoon.

Dead air.

Then, "I'm definitely *not* your mom."

"Oh—hi." It was Jill.

"I called three times. You at home?"

"No . . . I mean, yes. At the boat."

"Well . . . I wanted to say I'm sorry. For getting mad."

"No," he said, "it was my fault." Ben picked up his backpack, walked out onto the catwalk between the slips, and stepped up onto the deck of the boat.

"Yes, I agree—it was *completely* your fault," she said, and he could hear the smile in her voice. "Still, I shouldn't have gotten all huffy and stupid."

"Right," he added, "*completely* stupid, really."

"So," she said.

"So," he replied.

Ben had his key out now, and he opened the hatch and took three steps down into the galley, the tiny kitchen of the sailboat.

She said, "Could you do something for me?"

"That depends," he said.

"Send me the words from both sides of the coin in a text. Or an e-mail. Okay?"

"How come?"

"I want to see the exact words again, really look at them. And do some more thinking. And I'm going to look through all the stuff my mom collected about that company during the hearings. Just to see who we're up against here."

"Whoa," said Ben. "'Who *we're* up against'? When did this turn into a 'we' thing?"

"When you showed me that coin. And when you said Mr. Keane would have trusted me. Except we both know he would have trusted me *more*—'cause I'm so naturally charming."

"And so humble, too."

"Right," said Jill. "I'm very proud of how humble I am."

Ben was in the saloon now, the main living area of the boat. He flopped onto the couch and put his feet up on the table that was bolted to the floor.

Smiling, he said, "Well, my bravery scares me sometimes, but I'll send you those words anyway."

"Good," said Jill. "And I'll meet you tomorrow morning at the corner of Jefferson and Atlantic."

"Right, because I'm so much fun to hang out with."

"I can deal," she said. "Seven forty-five, okay?"

"Yup. Bye."

"Bye."

Ben had barely closed his phone when it rang again.

He pushed talk, and using his most cheerful voice, he said, "Hi, Mom." Because this time it was really her.

"Hi, Ben. Just wanted to be sure you got home all right."

"It's seven blocks, Mom. I'm fine. I'm always fine."

Ignoring that, she said, "So, how's everything going?"

Ben dreaded this daily question. If his answer sounded too happy, she worried that he was hiding his true feelings, or worse, that he didn't miss her at all. And if he let on that he was upset or sad, sometimes she got super smotherly, or even weepy, and he *really* couldn't deal with that.

So, in a neutral tone, he said, "Everything's pretty good—school's going okay, and I'm really glad the weather's getting nicer. We have to plant the garden soon, y'know. So, yeah, everything's good. How's Nelson?"

Rats! he thought. Dumb question! He tried to think quick and change the subject, but it was too late.

His mom paused a second, and then there was a catch in her voice. "Poor thing hates it when you're gone—runs to the door with his tail wagging like mad, and when it's not you, he just mopes back to his bed. Hardly eats a bite all week long."

"Well, I'll be home Saturday, Mom. Can't wait to

be with you. So, give Nelson a pat, and tell him we're all okay."

"That's right." She sounded braver now. "That's right, sweetheart. Well, good to talk. And I'll call you tomorrow. And I'll see you on Saturday. And remember that I'm going to drive over to the sailing club at about one thirty. And after your race we'll go get something to eat before you come home."

"Right, and thanks for calling. Love you."

"I love you too, Ben. Bye."

"Bye, Mom."

On any other afternoon, a chat like that would have left Ben staring out a porthole for ten minutes, maybe longer, worrying about his mom and dad and everything else—like his first sailing race of the season. But not today.

Today he had to think about other things.

He had a mission now. Plus a partner.

Which reminded him that he had to text Jill the words from the coin.

And maybe make some plans for tomorrow. Because it wasn't going to be just another Friday at school. In one day, everything about the place had changed.

There was that word again—no way to avoid it. But maybe the changes could at least be controlled a little. Or maybe a lot—Duncan Oakes seemed to think it was possible. And important.

But he was dead and gone.

This job needed someone very much alive . . . and present.

And Ben knew who it had to be.

CHAPTER 8

War Zone

It was Friday morning, and Ben was deep in thought as he walked beside the harbor on his way to meet Jill. He was thinking about Thursday night with his dad aboard the *Tempus Fugit*, replaying it through his mind, almost word for word, moment by moment, starting as they made dinner together.

"So, Ben," his dad had asked, "how was school today?"

"Well, this old janitor gave me a secret gold coin, and he made me promise I'd keep the school from being destroyed. And then he died."

That's what he *hadn't* said. All that stuff was secret.

"Had a big social studies test, and I'm pretty sure I aced it."

That's what had come out. Which hadn't been much of a surprise.

But his dad had still said, "That's great!" Then added, "Pass me the oregano, will you?"

Ben wished he could have talked about the plans to tear down the school, and about his terrible nightmare. And especially about Mr. Keane's death. But he'd kept all those thoughts and feelings bottled up—a skill he knew he was getting too good at.

And he'd handed his dad the oregano.

Then his dad had asked, "So what do you think about Saturday's race—your class is sailing the Optimists, right?"

And thinking about it, Ben knew that question had rescued the evening. Because suddenly there was plenty of stuff that they both loved to talk about.

They analyzed the weather forecast—strong breeze from the west, low seventies, some afternoon sun—excellent conditions. For May. In the Atlantic.

And then there was the course: Would the race committee make it a two-buoy course, or would they lay out a triangle? Lots of possibilities.

"But I just bet," his dad had said, "what with the water temperature in the forties, it's probably going to be a short course—a forty-minute race, tops."

And Ben had agreed.

Over salad and warm bread and steaming plates of spaghetti and sauce, they talked about starting strategies, about the new sails the club had bought, and also about clothes.

"Does your wet suit still fit?" his dad had asked. "You'll need it out there, guaranteed."

"Actually, it's too small, so Mom got me a dry suit, weighs almost nothing. Should be great."

That had stopped the conversation cold.

"A *dry* suit? I don't know, Ben . . . there's nothing like a good wet suit right next to your skin when there's a stiff spray coming onboard. . . . But you'll just have to see how this other thing works, that's all. If it's lousy, then we'll go to the Swamp Shop and get you a new wet suit, okay?"

Walking along the harbor twelve hours later, there was one thing Ben wished he'd been able to tell his dad about the race. Because he hadn't told him that his mom was also coming to watch.

But maybe he already knew that. Ben was pretty

sure his mom and dad talked on the phone a lot. But he never really overheard them.

Thinking ahead to the race, he imagined taking first place. Because that would be something both his parents could feel happy about. Maybe they could even be happy about it together. Maybe they would remember how much they loved to go sailing together. And then that big summer trip to the Bahamas just might seem like a good idea again.

But Ben knew that was a long shot. A very long shot. Still . . .

After dinner he had gone to his room—a tiny cabin up in the bow of the boat. It was barely big enough for a single bunk with two drawers beneath it, and a tiny fold-down desk that could hold his laptop and one book at a time.

He'd spent the night working on a reading assignment—and also replying to the e-mails Jill kept sending him.

Way too much information, really.

She could be like that sometimes, obsessing about stuff. Like the time in fourth grade when they had worked together on a science fair project about the ozone layer. Jill had checked out five huge library

books, found half a dozen articles on the NASA and the NOAA websites, and even did a telephone interview with a professor at Endicott College—all to make a small tabletop display and give a four-minute oral presentation.

Still, all the little details she was finding out about the Tall Ships Ahoy! project might be useful, and he was glad she liked digging around for them.

The next morning Jill met him at the corner of Jefferson and Atlantic, and they began retracing their steps to school—except this morning they walked on the west side of the street. A strong east wind had come up overnight, and the larger waves showered the harborside path with a heavy spray of seawater.

Jill picked up where her e-mails had left off the night before. "So what did you think about that last batch of stuff I sent—sort of scary, don't you think?"

"Yeah, scary's the right word."

Jill's final e-mail had been about the Glennley Entertainment Group, the company that had bought the school property. In the past four years they had opened three new historical theme parks, and each time, they had crushed every bit of opposition from the local communities. These people were ruthless.

But Ben had been wondering about an earlier message Jill had sent him, the one about the captain's last will and testament. She had found a copy of the will in the handouts her mom had brought home from one of the public meetings. One quote had stuck in his mind: "If the town ever stops using the Oakes building and its grounds as a public school, then full ownership shall pass immediately to my direct heirs."

As they paused to let the spray die down from an unusually large wave, he said, "I don't see how the town overturned the captain's will. I thought a thing like that was impossible to change."

"But they didn't change it," said Jill. "They went around it. First the Glennley lawyers found the captain's heirs—about fifteen people. And then they got the town to make the heirs an offer: 'If you give up all your rights to the school property, the town will pay each of you *five hundred thousand dollars* right now; but if any of you refuse, then the building will go on being a school forever, and none of you will ever get a penny.' So all the great-great-great-great-great-great-great grandchildren of Captain Oakes sold out to the town. And then the town turned around and sold everything to the Glennley Group for *more* money—

like, thirty-five million dollars. And everything was nice and legal—even though they completely trashed the captain's will."

"*Thirty-five million bucks?* Really?"

Jill nodded. "That's the money they're using to build the new school."

"Sheesh—how do you fight people who've got that much money to throw around?"

"By being smarter," said Jill, without missing a beat. "And by learning stuff they don't know about yet. And that message on the coin? Captain Oakes must have figured something like this might happen— an attack. And he definitely wants us to look for something."

"Right," Ben said, "'on the upper deck.' Wherever that is."

They both fell silent as they crossed Washington Street and entered the school grounds. After about ten paces, they stopped short and then stared.

Off to their left, midway between a copper beech tree and a tall white oak, a woman wearing an orange safety vest and a blue hard hat was hammering a long wooden stake into the ground. And she had been busy—there were eight or ten others scat-

tered around the schoolyard. About a hundred yards
beyond her, a man dressed the same way was peer-
ing into something that looked like a telescope on a
yellow tripod. The woman dropped her hammer and
tied a strip of bright pink ribbon around the top of
the stake. Huge red *X* marks had been spray painted
onto most of the tree trunks.

"What's going on?" asked Jill.

"Surveyors," Ben said. "That PDF file you sent me, the diagram of the theme park? They're marking it out on the ground—the theater, the parking lots, the twin wharves—everything. Bulldozers and chainsaws come next." He unclenched one fist and pointed at the nearest stake. "*That* is the beginning of the end."

As they walked closer to the building, Jill said, "There was one e-mail I didn't send you last night. 'Cause I didn't want you to stay up all night worrying. It's about Lyman."

"What about him?"

"You know how nosy I am, right?"

Ben smiled. "The queen of nosiness."

Ignoring that, she said, "So I did some snooping. When my mom went to the town meeting last month, she got a booklet with a list of all the town employees. Lyman's full name is Jerroald F. Lyman."

"Gerald?" asked Ben.

"No, J-E-R-R-O-A-L-D—which is an odd spelling. And when I put his name into Google, it turns out that there is only *one* Jerroald F. Lyman in the whole United States. And . . . I found stuff."

Ben stopped and looked at her. "Like what?"

"He was born in St. Louis. He went to an expensive prep school in Chicago. He graduated from Stanford University, then got a business degree in Philadelphia. He owns a house in Newport and a condo in Florida, plus a sixty-foot sailboat. The guy's rich. But for the last four months, Jerroald F. Lyman has been living in a rented room at an apartment house in Edgeport, Massachusetts. And he's working as the assistant janitor. At *our* school. And I'm sure it's the same person—I found pictures."

Ben stared at her, his mouth open. "But if he—I mean—oh . . . *Oh!* He's a *spy!*"

She nodded. "That's what I figured too. He has to be working for Glennley."

Ben froze, then grabbed Jill's arm. "Mr. Keane! Do you think he told Lyman about the coin? And the principal—he has to know about Lyman too, right? That he's working for Glennley?" Ben noticed he still had her arm and quickly let go.

Jill shrugged. "All I know for sure? *We've* got to

watch out. Because Lyman's *real* job is to make sure nothing goes wrong with the deal. And it sounds like he's already suspicious of you—the way he questioned you yesterday. If he figures out that we're up to something, we'll lose the element of surprise. And he'll try to stop us."

"Right," Ben said, impressed with Jill all over again. "Except for one thing—we don't know what he's supposedly going to try to keep us from doing. Or finding." The sound of the surveyor's hammer started up again, sharp and jarring. With a grim smile he said, "But we're gonna figure it out. We have to."

"We shouldn't hang out at lunch," Jill said.

"Or talk in the halls where Lyman might see us," said Ben.

"So I'll see you in math."

"Right," he said. "But I'll set my phone to vibrate, and if you get any ideas, sneak me a text. And I'll do the same."

Jill smiled. "Good. See you later."

"And don't forget," Ben said. "Until they rip it down, it's like Captain Oakes said—this place belongs to *us*."

Brave talk. But as Ben followed Jill into the front

hall of the school, he felt like they were walking into a war zone.

But worse than that, he also started feeling like all this stuff was just plain crazy. Because, really—spies? And secrets? It seemed pretty far out, right there at the edge of nutsville.

On the other hand, what if Lyman was really dangerous? Maybe the smartest thing would be to put on the brakes right now—hard. And just not get mixed up in any of it. Whatever was going to happen to the school and the town, let it come.

But Ben knew he couldn't walk away, not now. Because stealing the school from the kids, and changing the whole town this way? It just wasn't *right*.

He stumbled on that word.

Right? What, was he suddenly some kind of superhero, deciding all on his own what was right for everybody else?

And as he started up the south staircase, he thought, Hey, look, everybody—here comes SCHOOL BOY, ready to battle the forces of evil!

He smiled at that thought, but only for a second.

Because a different truth hit him. Now there

were feelings involved, his feelings. Feelings about this town. And about his parents. Feelings about a dead janitor, and feelings about a funky old building at the edge of the sea. Even some feelings about Jill.

This little war wasn't just about right and wrong, not by a long shot.

Now it was personal.

CHAPTER 9

Research

Ben had library during second-period reading. He was supposed to be working on an author study about Jack London, and his partner was Robert Gerritt. Which meant it wasn't any fun. But that guy was determined to create the best author study in the history of the universe—so at least Ben was sure he'd get an A on the project, whether *he* did any work or not.

By the time Ben got to the library, Robert was already busy comparing three different encyclopedia articles. When Ben sat down, he looked up and gave him a big grin.

"Hey there, Pratt—had any good nightmares

today? Why don't you put your head down and take a little nap?"

Ben ignored him. Ever since first grade Robert had acted like he was in this giant competition with everyone else, especially Ben. For the past week he had been completely obnoxious, and Ben knew why—they both belonged to the Bluewater Sailing Club, and they both sailed in the intermediate league. With the first race coming up, Robert was trying to psych him out.

"So," Robert went on, "you heard the weather report for tomorrow? Supposed to be blowing fifteen to twenty knots at race time, west to east—perfect conditions for me to do some serious butt kicking. How many times you been out this season?"

"Just once," Ben said. "It was freezing."

"Aw, did your mommy forget to send along hot chocolate for her little Benny? I've been out four times, Pratt. Real sailors don't care about the cold— and I am *pumped* for this race!"

He thumped a fist on the table so hard that the librarian looked over at him with a frown. Robert was built like a football player, a good three inches taller and wider than Ben. But weight wasn't always an advantage out on the water.

Ben said nothing and opened his notebook.

A minute later Robert was busy taking notes again, and Ben slipped away from the table—to do some independent research.

He waited until Mrs. Sinclair wasn't surrounded by kids, then went over to her desk.

"Do we have any books here about the history of the school?"

"Yes, in fact, we do—just one." The librarian got up and led Ben to a small collection of books in the reference area. He reached for a big leather-bound book, but she stopped him and pulled it off the shelf herself.

"This book is quite old, so you'll have to be very careful. And you must sit right here with it. All right?"

"I'll be careful," he said. "I promise."

So she left him alone, and for the next half hour Ben was in another world.

The title of the book was *A Man of the Sea, A School for the Ages*, and inside the front cover was a pen-and-ink illustration of the way the building and the grounds had looked back when Captain

Oakes had his ships tied up out front. The building had been a warehouse then, so the picture showed teams of tough-looking men rolling barrels and carting bales of goods out the wide front doors and up wooden gangplanks onto the ships.

Chapter 1 was mostly Oakes family history. It also explained how Captain Oakes had made a lot of money shipping goods between America and England. When the War of Independence began, he gave command of his ships to the new American navy. There was that great painting of Captain Oakes in full uniform on the deck of a ship, the one that was hanging in the third-floor hallway of the school. Another painting showed a British warship firing at the town of Edgeport. The front of the Oakes Building had been hit by three cannonballs, but the walls were so thick that the place had barely been damaged.

After the war, and after he had been thanked by Congress and President George Washington himself, Captain Oakes got the idea of turning his huge warehouse into a school, a permanent contribution to the life of the town and the nation.

Ben skipped around in the book a lot,

mostly skimming. But the chapter he really got into was the one about the construction work. The whole inside of the warehouse building had been ripped out and then rebuilt to make classrooms, hallways, and offices. And in the center of the book, there was a page that unfolded twice into a huge sheet. It was covered with copies of the original drawings and plans for the school remodeling job.

The person who had drawn up the plans and then supervised the school construction was a ship's carpenter named John Vining. The name seemed familiar to Ben, but he didn't stop to think about it—too much to look at. The man was a good artist, and Ben especially loved the small drawings around the edges of the plan. There were sketches showing how each fireplace should look, how the granite blocks for the front steps should be stacked, even drawings of the new doorknobs and hinges.

One drawing showed how the staircase landings would look, and how the hand-rails would be shaped. And on paper, Ben

CAPTAIN OAKES

SCHOOL PLANS

upperdeck

Oak railing
staircase
looking down
from the
upper deck

noticed something he had never seen while hurrying up and down the actual staircases of the school each day—the balusters and handrails looked like they belonged on an old sailing ship, which made sense, of course. John Vining worked mostly on ships, not on buildings.

Ben's eye was drawn to the lower left corner of the large sheet. There was an especially clear drawing, and below it a carefully written note from the carpenter:

Oak railing staircase looking down from the upper deck

Ben almost jumped out of his chair, almost shouted, *The words on the coin!*

Of course—the captain and his carpenter were sailors! They wouldn't have talked about the first, second, or third floor—they would have said lower, middle, or upper *deck*—*"If attacked, look nor'-nor'east from amidships on the upper deck"*!

The reference area was tucked away behind the librarian's desk, so Ben got out his phone and lit up the camera. He zoomed in on the left corner of the large sheet, let the camera focus, and snapped an image. Then he sent the picture in a text to Jill.

He carefully refolded the large page, closed the book, stood up, and slipped it back into its place on the shelf. Then he walked around the end of the tall bookcase—and his heart nearly stopped.

It was Lyman. He was washing one of the large windows that surrounded the library workroom, a spray bottle in one hand and a rag in the other.

Ben looked away quickly, his head spinning. Did Lyman have his class schedule? And that book—did he see Ben take that picture? Maybe he knew all about the coin, knew it was in his pocket right this minute!

Ben made himself walk casually back to where Robert was slaving away. He made himself sit and open his notebook to his report, made himself put his pen on the paper and write some words, one after another. He even made himself breathe slowly.

He looked calm, but inside he was churning. He couldn't wait to get to math class next period. He'd be able to tell Jill about the book and explain that picture he'd sent.

Unless Lyman followed him.

And another reason he couldn't wait to get to math class? It was up on the third floor—*the upper deck!*

CHAPTER 10

Rose on the Floor

Ben didn't believe in ghosts. At least, he didn't think he did. But as he burst out of the library and headed for the south staircase, it felt like something was directing him, making him see things, making him think things. It was just his imagination . . . probably.

He passed the framed parchment map of Edgeport on the wall outside the office just as he had a thousand times before—except this time he saw the town where Captain Oakes had grown up, lived a long life, and then died.

As he waited with a bunch of other kids near the stairs, he imagined himself surrounded by boys in knee breeches and homespun shirts, and girls wearing long, plain dresses. He heard their feet on the floorboards—heavy hobnail boots and square-toed shoes with buckles. He imagined horses snorting at the hitching posts out back, and wooden ships creaking against the seawall out front.

And as he went up the stairs, every landing looked like the afterdeck of a frigate. He noticed the curved oak posts rising up along the side walls to support the floor joists, noticed how the floor planks were as thick as the deck of a ship, resting on chestnut beams that could have survived a direct hit from a cannonball—which they actually did.

It was the sort of woodwork built to endure the ice storms and winds of the North Atlantic. And more than two hundred years later, after weathering the bumps and pulls and thumps of tens of thousands of kids, none of the railings wobbled, none of the floors creaked or sagged. This place had been built for rough weather, and it was still shipshape.

When Ben got to the third floor, he spotted Jill near the math room. He did a quick scan for the janitor—all clear. So he walked over.

"I got the picture you sent," she said. "It's too small. What is it?"

Ben quickly explained what he'd discovered, expecting her to be impressed.

With her head tilted to one side, she said, "Are you sure?"

"Absolutely."

Ben pointed at the railing around the staircase. "That's it right there—the woodwork from the drawing I sent. And the carpenter's note said it was on the upper deck."

"Okay . . . so if this *is* the upper deck, then how do you find 'amidships'?"

Ben pulled out a sketch he had made during his last few minutes in the library.

"Here's the shoreline to the east, and this is the original school building, which is basically a rectangle. And anywhere along this east-west line through the center of the building would be 'amidships.' Plus anywhere along *this* north-south center line could also be called amidships. But *true* amidships would be right where those two lines cross. And if we find that spot, then we use a compass and strike a line north-northeast, and see what we find."

"I think there's one over there. On the floor."

"What? What are you talking about?"

"A compass," Jill said. "Just outside the girls' room. There's a round thingie on the floor with an arrow and a capital *N*. So that's a compass, right?"

"Be right back." Ben rushed straight for the girls' room, but about six feet away he stopped. Four girls were standing there, and they quit talking and stared at him. He didn't dare get closer.

But he went to the wall opposite the doorway and looked north along the hall, then south toward the staircase where he'd left Jill. And he was pretty sure he was standing amidships.

He hurried back to Jill, who had clearly enjoyed his embarrassment at the girls' room door. He ignored her grin.

"So, when you say this compass is 'on the floor,' what do you mean?"

Jill got serious again. "It's not really *on* the floor, it's more like it's *in* the floor, right in the wood. A metal circle about as big as a necklace. And the arrow sticking through it, and—"

"That's a compass rose! And the carpenter must have put it there as a clue, a marker. And now we just have to—"

The school bell rang, the first of three clangs, and the kids still in the hall scrambled for their classrooms.

Ben and Jill spent the next fifty-four minutes on opposite sides of the math lab. It was a review day for the big state test, so there were nonstop drills and timed problems. Ben spent a lot of time hunching down over his workbook or staring at the explanations on the chalkboard, and he asked Mrs. Burmeister at least ten questions. Math wasn't his best subject.

When class ended, Jill hurried up to Ben out in the hall and handed him a piece of paper.

"It looks sort of like this, the compass rose."

He barely glanced at it. "Good. C'mon, we've got to go talk to Mrs. Hinman."

"Now? How come?"

Ben was already headed for their social studies classroom. "You'll see. Just nod and smile till you catch on."

The teacher was gathering her things to go to lunch, and Ben smiled when she looked up at him. "Hi, Mrs. Hinman. I know this is a bad time to talk, but this'll only take a second. If Jill and I wanted to do a special project about the history of Oakes School, would you help us out? Because we'd need permission to be in the building before classes, and probably after school too. For research."

Jill nodded. And smiled.

He went on, "And we'll have to work on it at least a couple of weeks."

Jill smiled again. And nodded.

Mrs. Hinman pursed her lips and eyed the two students suspiciously. "You want to start a special project? This close to the end of the year?"

Jill nodded, then quickly said, "Really, it was my idea. Because my social studies grade isn't so great. So

if we could get some extra-credit points, that would be great, like, maybe if we gave a report to the class before the end of school?"

From right behind them a voice said, "Yeah, a report. For extra credit."

Jill and Ben jerked their heads to look, and it was Robert Gerritt, a serious look on his face, all business.

Turning quickly back to the teacher, Ben said, "Actually, Jill and I wanted to work on this by ourselves, and we—"

"No fair," said Robert, shaking his head. "If it's an extra-credit project, I should be able to work on it too, right? And I want to do my own part, so I get a separate grade. Yeah—maybe I could make my part of the report like a documentary movie or something. So I'll get graded for my own work."

Mrs. Hinman was already motioning them toward the door. "This all sounds fine. And Robert's right—besides, it's probably a bigger project than you and Jill think, so there'll be plenty for everyone to do. I'll help get you started, and I'll also ask Mrs. Sinclair if you can use the library before and after school. She's in early, and there's always someone there after school."

Ben didn't want to seem upset about Robert, so he said, "That'll be great, but could we have a meeting about it today? 'Cause we really want to get started. Like, maybe after lunch?"

The teacher shook her head. "Not today—I've got playground duty. I'll mention it to Mrs. Sinclair after school, and then we can all talk again on Monday. Now off you go," and she herded them into the hall, pulled her door shut, and then slipped past and hurried down the south stairwell.

Robert said, "This is great, huh? Sorry to butt in and everything, but I really need the extra points. For my grade."

Ben nodded and tried to smile. Right, for his grade. He probably wanted to get an A++ in social studies, instead of just an A+. This guy was a royal pain. Plus, he was already stuck with Robert on that Jack London report. The idea of having to work with him on something else was almost more than Ben could bear.

"So, talk to you losers later, okay? I've got to catch up with Mrs. Hinman and ask her a question." And he dashed away down the stairs, his footsteps echoing in the empty hallway.

Ben glared at Jill. "You had to get all clever and ask for extra credit. Now we've got to deal with *him*," and he jerked his thumb toward the stairwell.

Jill didn't blink. "Mrs. Hinman thought you were nuts, and she was right. Nobody just walks up to a teacher and asks for some extra schoolwork. So my *cleverness* just saved your half-baked idea. And don't worry about Robert—he could even be useful. As a distraction."

Ben knew Jill was right—about everything. But he gave her a disgusted look anyway and headed for the stairs.

"Where are you going?" she said.

"Duh—lunch."

"Not me." Jill looked around, then turned and started walking north. "I'm going to the girls' room—amidships." She glanced back at Ben with a smile. "Coming?"

CHAPTER 11

Artifacts

The compass rose was just as Jill had described it, an arrow through a ring of brass, set into a wide oak floorboard. It was worn bright and shiny by the constant foot traffic at the girls' room door.

"How do you find north-northeast?" she whispered.

"Think of this circle like it's a clock. North is where twelve o'clock would be. East is where the three would be, which is like fifteen minutes past twelve. Northeast is halfway between north and east, which would be like seven and a half minutes past twelve. And *north*-northeast is half of that—which would be like about four minutes after the twelve. Get it?"

Jill nodded. "So we use this to aim with, and then we look for something, right?"

"I think so," said Ben. "But we'll need . . ."

Footsteps, coming up the south staircase—*tap-tap-tap-tap* . . . but they stayed on the second floor, and gradually faded away.

"We'll need what?" whispered Jill.

"A long string to make a straight line. Or a laser pointer."

Jill's eyes crinkled. "Promise not to laugh?"

"What?"

She was already digging in the outer pocket of her book bag. "I've got dental floss—just be glad *your* mom never worked for a dentist."

Ben grinned. "And it's the minty kind—my favorite!"

A minute later Ben held one end of the floss

at the right spot on the compass rose, and Jill had unreeled the spool down the hallway.

Ben motioned her to move right, and then to the left, and finally she was up against the wall about thirty feet away, north-northeast. The smell of mint filled the air.

"Okay," he whispered. "Stay right there."

He walked slowly along the path marked by the line of floss, not sure what he was looking for. A loose floorboard? There weren't any. A special mark? Or a group of nails that made a pattern? Nothing jumped out at him.

When he got to where Jill stood, he looked at the floor, examined the wall above the end of the line, and scanned the whole area for several feet on either side. Still nothing.

"Here," he whispered. "Just put the floss down. Help me look."

Walking to the other side of the hall, they stood almost in front of the tall portrait of Captain Oakes, and looked back at where the little white plastic box marked the spot. Again, nothing.

Then Ben grabbed Jill's arm, and she jumped. "*Ow!* What?"

"The molding—the boards along the floor! See?"

Jill shook her head.

"Look at how *long* the molding boards are. Ten feet or twelve feet long, maybe, and then there's a break, and a new board starts. Look at the seams—see?"

Jill slowly nodded. "Yeah . . . and?"

"And now look just to the right of the floss. See that short board—about eight inches long?"

"Yeah . . . ?"

"If a carpenter was running out of longer boards, the little pieces would go nearer the ends, or close to a corner where they wouldn't show as much. You wouldn't stick a short piece in the middle like that—unless there was a reason for it. C'mon!"

Up close, Ben saw that the brown varnish coating the baseboard was checked and cracked. And thick.

The seams on both ends of the short piece were filled with it.

Ben grabbed a stainless steel ruler from his backpack and pushed the sharp corner of the thin metal into the crack on the left side of the short molding board. Then he worked it upward with a sawing motion. The dried varnish crumbled to dust, leaving a thin seam. He did the same to the crack on the right side of the board. Along the top of the beveled board, pale green paint filled the crack between the wood and the wall, and Ben used the ruler to clean that out as well.

"Now what?" whispered Jill.

"Move over a little so there's better light."

Jill moved, and then she bent down close to the molding. "Is that anything?" She pointed at a nick on the top edge of the board.

"Probably not," said Ben. There were dings and dents all over the place. He took a closer look. "Actually . . . you're right. Looks like someone made a tiny V there, like with a chisel or a knife. On purpose."

"So it's a pointer?" Jill asked.

Ben nodded. "It is—I'm sure of it."

"Here," Jill said, and took the ruler from his hand,

slipping it down between the wall and the wood right at the V mark. She pushed the ruler in three inches and then stopped.

"What?" whispered Ben.

"It's hitting something . . . Feels like metal."

The thin stainless steel flexed as Jill increased the pressure. "I'm going to ruin this thing."

"Go ahead and push."

Her knuckles were white, her face flushed with effort as she pushed and pried with the ruler. Then *click*—the piece of baseboard moved forward, pulling away from the wall almost a half an inch. Using both hands, she put her fingertips along the top of the board and pulled.

The front edge of the baseboard stayed put as the whole piece tipped forward—two small brass hinges held the bottom to the floor. Ben saw a thin strip of metal sticking out from the wall, which matched up with a slot in the wood. "Very cool."

"Look!" Jill whispered.

On the inside surface of the board was a big iron key. It was actually *in* the wood, embedded in its own perfectly carved outline.

"Go ahead—take it out."

Jill used the ruler to pry at the key, first one end, then the other, until it came free of the board.

"It's *heavy!*"

Jill turned the key over in her hand, and they both saw some writing scratched into the metal, rusty but legible:

USE ONLY IF YOU MUST

Ben turned back to look at the wall, then nudged Jill. There was a cut in the plaster wall that the molding had covered, a narrow slot about two inches high and six inches wide. He put three fingers into the opening and felt around, then pulled them out, covered with thick dust. Also a few mouse droppings.

"*Gross!*" said Jill.

"Let me have the ruler."

Ben pushed the strip of metal into the bottom edge of the slot, then slid it from side to side, using it like a spatula. Then he reached in again and removed a length of pine board about five inches square, dusty and dark brown with age.

"A piece of wood?" whispered Jill.

"Looks that way," he said, "except it's too heavy. And look—here on the edge of the board. There's a—"

Ben froze, held up his hand.

A sound. From the north staircase. Then another— the unmistakable clank of a large metal bucket. And heavy footsteps on the stairs. Coming up.

"*Lyman!*"

Jill jammed the key into her pocket, and Ben shoved the tilted baseboard back into place—*click*.

They scrambled to their feet, and as she grabbed up the dental floss, he dashed to his backpack and slipped the pine board inside. In five seconds they were skimming down the south stairs.

When they got to the first floor, Ben pointed. "Go into the girls' room."

Jill gave him an odd look.

"Just do it," he said. "Five seconds."

He ducked into the boys' room and washed the dust off his hands. When he came out, they hurried along the deserted central hallway of the old building and went through the causeway into the Annex.

Ben had the feeling Lyman was watching them, and just before they reached a corner he took a quick look over his shoulder. No one.

Mrs. Flagg stopped them inside the door of the cafeteria. "You're late for lunch."

Ben nodded. "I went to the restroom."

Jill said, "Me too."

The teacher waved them on.

Ben bought a carton of chocolate milk, and Jill got some plain 2 percent. Before she headed for the food line, Ben said, "So . . . don't lose that key, and don't unlock anything without me, okay?"

She smiled. "Not a chance. And don't even *think* about looking at that hunk of wood unless I'm there too."

"Fair enough."

Jill arched an eyebrow at him. "Anything else?"

"Nope. Except I think this might be the most fun I've had at school since kindergarten."

Jill laughed. "Me too. See you at two forty-five, okay?"

"Yeah, but let's meet just beyond the school grounds. In case anyone's watching."

Ben went and sat at his usual lunch spot with Luke, Bill, and Gabe, and right away Bill said, "Hey—you and Jill, huh? Nice."

Ben shook his head. "Nah, it's not like that. We're working on a project for Hinman's class."

He looked away and took a big bite of his peanut butter sandwich, and that stopped the public discussion of his personal life.

But Ben certainly didn't stop thinking about it, along with a hundred other things.

And he smiled to himself—just a little.

CHAPTER 12

Finders, Keepers

"I'm not supposed to be here, right?"

Ben nodded. "My dad usually doesn't let me have friends on the boat when he's out. But if it's only for a few minutes, it'll be okay."

Jill sat down on the worn couch in the main cabin and looked up at the row of oblong portholes that rimmed the small room. Bright afternoon sun threw patterns onto the curved wall across from her, and the steady rocking of the boat put them in motion.

"Doesn't it drive you crazy, how everything's always moving around?"

"You get used to it."

"But it's so *small* in here. . . . I mean, I guess I knew that, 'cause the whole boat's not very long."

"Or wide," added Ben. "But you get used to that, too. And I like small spaces anyway. My room at home isn't big either . . . At my mom's house, I mean."

"How long have you had this boat?"

"Not really sure. My dad got it before I was born, even before my folks got married. He bought it real cheap and fixed it up. My mom says Dad loves the boat more than both of us put together." He paused a second, then added, "But that's not true."

After an awkward moment, Ben said, "So, ready for the big unveiling?"

"Absolutely."

Ben pulled up the side leaf on the table in front of Jill, and it clicked into place. He zipped open his book bag, took out the square piece of pine board, then handed it to her.

"See what I mean, how it feels too heavy to be just wood? 'Cause white pine is really light, especially when it's old and dry like this. And you see that thin line all around the edge?"

"Yeah . . ."

Ben got up, took three steps to the galley, opened

a drawer by the sink, and got out a small paring knife. Back at the table, he took the piece of wood from Jill and used the slim blade to gently pry at the crack— which got wider. It only took a minute before the board came apart into two halves.

And inside there was a square sheet of copper, tacked into place at the corners—and there was writing, scribed into the metal.

"Look at that!" Jill breathed.

Ben nodded, squinting at the tiny words. The copper was the color of an old penny. "We need more light."

He moved the tablet into a patch of direct sun, and they each read the words silently:

If you have found this message on purpose, then an evil day besets us
for you must have been shown, the coin with its words of warning
Captain Oakes has given this school to us, to the Children
but he feared others would one day try to take it away
It is a day he prepared for, and that day is come.
He prepared five safeguards to help us in our self defense—
hidden, lest they be too easily found and put to wrong use:
After five bells sound, time to sit down
After four times four, tread up one more

If you have found this message on purpose, then an evil day besets us,
for you must have been shown the coin with its words of warning.
Captain Oakes has given this school to us, to the children,
but he feared others would one day try to take it away.
It is a day he prepared for, and that day is come.
He prepared five safeguards to help us in our self-defense—
hidden, lest they be too easily found and put to wrong use:
After five bells sound, time to sit down.
After four times four, tread up one more.
After three hooks pass, one will be brass.
After two tides spin, a man walks in.
After one still star, horizons afar.
You must seek each safeguard in order, from five to one,
and you must use <u>only</u> what is needed—
leave things unneeded undisturbed.
Above all, seek the final safeguard ONLY IF YOU MUST—
for once the last is found, our school will change forever.
You must now swear a most fearsome oath of secrecy,
and promise to defend this school—
for it truly is this school that defends us all
from ignorance, poverty, and tyranny.
Though we may be dead and buried as you read these words,
our duties here live on, and honor demands that you serve alongside us.
We the children will always be
the Keepers of the School.

Thomas Vining   Louis Hendley   Abigail Baynes
Hereupon have we signed with our own hands on this day,
April 12, 1791

Jill finished reading first. "Wow! So . . . like, these are *students* who wrote this? That's amazing."

Ben nodded. "Yeah, it is . . . Hey!" He tapped excitedly on the copper plate. "See this kid's last name? It's the same as the man who drew up the plans, the ones for the school—I bet it's his father. So . . . that means these kids weren't doing stuff all on their own. Which makes it a little less amazing."

He picked up the lid that had covered the writing and turned it over a few times. "And making a thing like this? Serious woodworking skills. Same with that hiding place. But . . . if it was actually the captain and his carpenter planning everything, how come they brought the kids into it?"

Jill shrugged. "Maybe Captain Oakes didn't trust anybody except carpenters, janitors, and kids."

"But kids don't stay kids very long—they grow up, right?"

"Yeah," said Jill, "but don't forget the weirdo factor. Maybe we shouldn't count on finding a whole lot of logic in what the captain was doing. This is the same guy who had himself buried in the middle of the school playground."

"Good point." Ben got out his laptop, opened a

new document, and began to type, copying the words from the metal plate.

Jill stood up and hooked her backpack over one shoulder. "Well, hate to say it, but I've got to head for home now. Before my mom sends the police out looking for me. Or the coast guard. But I'm glad I got to see that message. And your boat. It's a very cool place to live." She walked into the galley.

Ben looked up from the keyboard. "Can't you stick around awhile? So we can try to figure out what some of this stuff means? Just call your mom and tell her where you are."

"I . . . don't think that's a good idea. She's pretty old-fashioned—doesn't want me at somebody's house if the parents aren't home. And I know she'd start asking questions. About everything. So I'd better just go."

"Well, wait a minute and I'll walk with you."

"That's okay, you don't have to," she said.

"I know . . . but I've got to go get some milk. At the Scuttle Mart."

Actually, Ben thought he might ask Jill to come watch his race Saturday afternoon. Except he didn't know if she'd want to. She hadn't seemed that interested when they'd talked about sailing on Thursday.

But maybe he'd at least mention it again. . . .

Five minutes later they were walking up the slanted gangway toward the security booth. As they passed it, Ben smiled and waved at the guard behind the sliding door. And when he did, the man opened the glass and motioned him over.

"Hi, Kevin."

"Hey there, Ben—didn't see you go by earlier. This is for your dad—it's from the fella who stopped by this morning. Said they could talk again tomorrow."

He handed Ben a business card: JACKSON SWERDLING, YACHT BROKER. There was a post office box in Charlestown and a couple of phone numbers.

"So . . . this guy was looking at our boat?"

"Yup, a little before eleven. Took some measurements. Said he's already got a buyer."

What? Ben was stunned. He barely managed to say, "Thanks," as he turned away. He walked stiffly to where Jill was waiting.

"What's wrong?"

He gave her the card. "My dad. He's—he's selling the boat. Just like that."

"Would he *do* that?" Jill asked.

"What, sell it? Sure, why not? It's *his* boat," Ben

snapped. "He can do whatever he wants with the thing."

"No," said Jill. "I mean, would he ever do something this major, just like that? Without even mentioning it, without telling you *anything*?"

"Who knows? And it doesn't matter, because he's already got some broker working on—"

She cut him off. "I'll be back in a second."

"What? Where are you going

"Just wait here, okay?"

Jill trotted back over to the security shed and tapped on the glass. Kevin smiled at her as he slid the window open, and then listened while she talked. He nodded a few times, a puzzled look on his face. Jill talked some more, and the guard nodded again. Then he smiled and waved so long, and she turned and hurried back over to Ben.

"What was all that about?" he asked.

"The yacht broker. I had some questions about him—like, 'Was he really tall?' And, 'Was he wearing a dark suit?' And, 'Did he have a long, thin face, with deep-set eyes, dark hair parted almost in the middle?' And the answer to all those questions was *yes*. So I'll bet you anything there *wasn't* a yacht broker looking at your sailboat today."

"Wait . . . *no*. You think it was *Lyman*? Here at our boat?"

Jill nodded. "I'm sure of it. I described him exactly, and everything matches up. It's too big a coincidence. He was here."

Ben's face went pale, and he felt like he was going to fall over.

"Let's walk, okay?" Jill steered him by his elbow off the marina's planks and onto the harborside path. "Take some deep breaths."

"I'm okay," he said, pulling his arm away. "It just creeps me out, that's all. I mean . . . do you think he went *inside*? Like, in my cabin?"

"I don't know. Just keep walking."

"But . . . how did you even *think* it might have been Lyman?"

"Mostly a hunch. But it was also what you said—

about how your dad loves that boat. I mean, why would he sell it, especially if he needs to live on it right now? And then not even mention it to you? Doesn't make sense. Plus, I've had Lyman on the brain ever since I found all that stuff online."

"How come he's so focused on me? Like, what's he looking for—is it just the coin?"

"I don't think he knows anything for sure, which probably drives him crazy. We know Mr. Keane told Lyman *something*, and whatever that was, Lyman got worried—which means the people who hired him got worried too. So he was watching Keane like a hawk, trying to find out if he really knew about something that could mess up the deal. And suddenly the old janitor dies, and who's the last person he talks to?"

"Me," said Ben.

"Exactly—and Lyman knows that Keane might have told you something, or even handed you something, which, of course, he actually did. And then after school yesterday, when Lyman asked you about your time with the old guy? You acted funny, so he got even more suspicious. And now *you're* his new target—congratulations." Jill glanced casually back over her shoulder. "He might even be watching us right now. And he could have been listening, too."

Ben stopped and whipped around to face her. "*Microphones*—on the boat! He could have heard everything we just said!"

Again, Jill gently steered him forward. "Can't do anything about that now. If it happened, it happened. And he would know that we found something— but he doesn't know what. Or where we got it. And we didn't read the message out loud. So we need to keep acting like nothing's weird, nothing's wrong, like we have no idea he was here, or that he's even watching you. And if your place *is* bugged, and we *know* it is, but he doesn't know *we* know—then that's good for us. Weird . . . and a little scary, but good."

Ben was walking so fast now that Jill almost had to trot to keep up. "But how did he get over here this morning? He was at school. I *saw* him in the library during second period."

"There was a wake for Mr. Keane today from eleven to one. And his funeral's on Monday. You need to pay attention to the announcements during home-room, Benjamin. And slow down."

They walked the rest of the way to Jefferson Street in silence.

When they got to the door of her building, Jill said, "If you want to come in for a while, you can. Until your dad gets home."

Ben put his hands in his pockets, and his right hand closed around the gold coin. "No, I'm okay. It's not like Lyman's a maniac or something. Just a skinny industrial spy. And we know more about him than he knows about us." Ben was quiet a few seconds. "Is there any way he could tap into my e-mail?"

She shook her head. "Not if your firewall's on."

"Good. 'Cause I won't be calling you from the boat—unless we work out something that we *want* him to hear. But . . . we don't really know yet if he's listening—I mean, we really don't know much of *anything* right now." Ben shook his head. "Maybe we're making way too much out of all this stuff." Another few moments of silence, and then he spoke more slowly. "But I don't think so. If there was even a tiny possibility that something could stop this deal, that would be a nightmare for the Glennley company—it'd cost them millions, probably cause huge lawsuits, all kinds of trouble. So if there's *any* chance something could wreck it, they'd *have* to investigate. Even if it's just a couple of kids poking around."

"Well, *I* think we're onto something big here," said Jill, a grim smile on her face. "And we're not just a couple of nosy kids, either. Because we're not in this thing alone, not by a long shot."

"Yeah," Ben said with a smirk, "there's the two of us, the three dead kids, the dead janitor, and the dead sea captain—quite a team."

"Be serious, Ben."

"Oh, I am—really. I'm being very serious. But you have to admit, this is completely strange. And we're just barely getting started."

Jill shifted gears, thinking ahead. "So, be sure to e-mail me the text from that copper plate this weekend, okay?"

"Yup. And I expect you to have all five of those clues completely decoded by Monday morning."

"Very funny." Jill paused a moment, then looked Ben in the eye. "And we're not telling *anybody* about this, right?"

"Absolutely," he said. "At this moment, there are exactly two Keepers of the School—you and me."

"That's right," said Jill. "'We the children.'"

CHAPTER 13

Clean Start

It was one fifteen on Saturday afternoon, and Ben was sorry he hadn't invited Jill to come watch him race. The conditions were perfect—a brisk offshore breeze blowing from the west, a mix of clouds and sun, a light chop to the water, and almost no swell.

Twenty-four kids had signed up to race, but since a lot of them didn't own their own boats, there would be two races with twelve boats each. Ben was glad to see his name on the list for the first race. But Robert Gerritt was in the first race too, so there was no way to avoid a direct showdown today. Among the intermediate sailors he and Robert had the most experience, and last season's race tally had ended in a draw—seven first-place finishes for each of them. And seven second-place finishes.

They were racing in Optimists today, which was fine with Ben. Some other local clubs had their intermediate sailors race in 420s, which needed a crew of two. Ben liked the stubby little dinghy because it had a crew of one—him.

The club owned ten Optimists, and like the other the kids who didn't have boats of their own, Ben pulled a number from a bag for his boat assignment. He drew number nine, one of the newer ones, so its hull still had a smooth factory finish on it—and smoother meant faster. Sweet.

At the gear inspection on the beach, Ben kept busy with his own preparations, and he was glad Robert was about thirty yards away. He had his own boat this year, a brand-new one, and he'd made a point of telling Ben all about it. But as he worked, Ben couldn't avoid noticing Robert's boat. It was the only boat on the beach with the big Olympic-size letters and numbers on its sail—USA 222.

Since the water was just forty-three degrees, the race adviser walked around and double-checked each boat and also made sure that each sailor had warm, waterproof clothes. And even if you had aced the swimming test, a bright orange life vest was mandatory.

Ben tied down each of the three air bags in his boat and then tightened the hiking straps, the broad nylon bands he'd have to hook his feet under when he leaned out over the edge of the boat—and by the looks of the whitecaps on the waves out there, there'd be plenty of that today. Even though the wind felt chilly and it was beginning to cloud up, his new dry suit kept him so warm that he had to unzip his jacket. But it would feel a lot different out on open water. Still, he felt like he was ready for anything, especially since his dad had surprised him at breakfast today with some new insulated gloves.

As he pulled on the halyard line to raise the sail, he glanced up the beach toward the clubhouse. He spotted his dad's red windbreaker right away, up on the deck outside the dining room. And then he saw his mom, too—except she was out near the end of the pier.

He felt a stab of disappointment. Last summer they had watched every race together. He snapped his eyes back to the mast and gave a sharp yank on

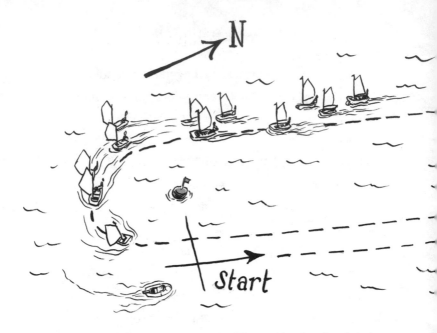

the halyard, then fastened the line. And as he did the final tuning of the sail, he pushed everything else out of his mind. It was race time.

Today's course was simple, and Ben fixed it in his mind as the race adviser helped him push his boat off from the beach and fasten his tiller in place.

There were just two markers out there, and they were only about a quarter mile apart. After crossing the start line at the southern buoy, he'd have to sail to the northern marker, turn his boat around into the wind, scoot back and go around the southern marker, make one more run up to the northern buoy,

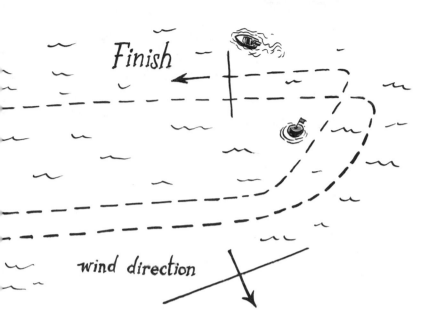

Finish

wind direction

and sail round it a second time to reach the finish line.

The race officers were watching and scoring the race today from two motorboats, one near the start line and the other near the finish. Some of the spectators were out on the water in their own boats, well outside the course, but still a lot closer to the action than the parents and friends watching through binoculars from the shore. Like his parents.

As his little boat slapped and skipped its way toward the starting buoy, Ben felt a sudden surge of happiness. He loved being out on the water. And he also loved that his mom and dad were watching him, both of them. So what if they weren't standing side by side? This was the first thing they'd done together since they separated. Well, sort of together. Which was tons better than not together at all.

But he couldn't let himself think anything about that. Or hope anything. He pushed it all out of his mind again, because right now, he had to make a clean start.

He yanked in on the sheet, the rope attached to the boom along the bottom of the sail, pulling in until it almost touched his chin. His boat shot forward into a gap just to the right of the southern buoy. The wind made the boat tip up, so Ben dug his toes down under the hiking straps and leaned way out over the edge. Freezing spray stung his eyes and water ran down his neck, but the hull leveled off and sliced a sharp line through the waves—and that was all that mattered.

Ben was on a port tack, and sure enough, someone screamed, "Starboard!" demanding the right of way. He adjusted his tiller and grazed past the other boat with about a foot to spare. Close call, but it was always like that at the start of a race, especially in a strong breeze.

He took a quick look over his shoulder at the race officer's motorboat to see which flags were up—the Optimist class flag, plus the Preparatory flag, a white rectangle on a blue field. Which meant there were about four minutes until the start. The next long blast from the air horn would be at the one-minute mark, when the Prep flag was lowered.

Crunch time. Ben knew this race would probably be won or lost right at the starting line. He had to be crossing the line *just after* the Optimist flag was dropped and the air horn sounded the start. Cross that line one second too soon, and he'd have to take a penalty turn, which meant he'd play catch-up for the rest of the race.

As he battled the eleven other kids who were trying to do exactly the same thing on the same small patch of water, Ben felt like he was in a bumper car arena—except flapping sails kept blocking his vision, and a collision would mean a penalty.

Ben gritted his teeth to keep them from chattering, let the sheet run loose, and jammed the tiller stick hard to starboard, which whipped the boat into a quick turn, more than ninety degrees. He scrambled to the other side of the boat, then ducked as the boom went zipping by above his head. He took up the slack on the sheet rope, and now he was on a starboard tack. He eyed the little flag at the top of his mast to check the wind direction again, then looked under the sail to see if Robert was anywhere nearby. Sure enough, boat number 222 was also running on a starboard tack, just to leeward and about three lengths ahead.

Robert must have spotted him, too, because he yelled out across the water. "Hey, Pratt—you might as well head for shore. I *own* this course!"

Talk like that could have earned Robert a penalty, but Ben ignored it. He watched his trim, watched his course, watched the round red buoy, watched the boats milling around him on all sides. Everybody was trying to be in the right spot at the right moment for that flying start across the line.

He grabbed the scoop bailer and tossed a few quick quarts of water overboard, just as a big wave sloshed another blast across the bow.

His shoes were full of seawater and his feet felt like Popsicles. But if freezing slosh was the price he had to pay for a great wind, bring it on—this was sailing!

Ben let his boat slip a little downwind, then swung it around again and beat toward shore, looped back again toward the starting buoy, and then pulled it around once more, now sailing away from the starting line.

Rheeeeehp! At the long blast from the air horn, Ben punched the waterproof timer strapped to his wrist, then looked astern and got a fix on that beautiful big red buoy. His timer was counting down from sixty, and when it reached thirty seconds, he'd swing the boat around one last time and shoot northward again, reaching the line just as the Optimist flag dropped—at least that was the plan. Gusts and lulls, boats windward and alee, right-of-way conflicts—so many things could mess up his start. Not to mention Robert.

Thirty-two, thirty-one, thirty . . . "Ready about!"

He jammed his tiller, released the sheet, and executed a perfect turn. Now he had a clear shot, straight to the line, and just to leeward of the first

mark. He gave the sheet a tug, adjusted the tiller,
and zipped toward the start.

"Clear, clear! Number nine, keep clear there!"

Ben ducked his head to see beneath his sail
Number 222—Robert! He had gotten his boat just
barely even with Ben's. And since Robert had the
leeward boat, under Rule Eleven, Ben had to give
way in order to keep clear. A flash of anger made him

wish he could draw a sword from his belt and shout, *I'll see your blood for this, you scurvy cur!* But this was civilized sailing, so Ben pushed his tiller away, barely a twitch, knocking his boat a few degrees off its perfect course.

And the moment he did that, Robert edged his boat up close underneath him again and yelled the same thing.

"Clear! Keep clear!"

Again Ben had to give way, steering that much closer toward the marker buoy. He knew exactly what Robert was doing—two more adjustments like that, and Ben would be forced to either come about or sail to the left side of the buoy—a disqualified start.

"Clear! Keep clear!" Robert bellowed, edging his boat up so close underneath him that if Ben had let out his sail, the boom would have whacked Robert on the back—which he was very tempted to do.

Ben gave way again, but this time he pushed his tiller far enough so that a big gulp of wind spilled off his sail, and instantly Robert's boat slipped ahead by a full length. Then Ben pulled his tiller back the other way, cinched up his sheet, and five seconds later *he* was the one in the leeward spot, just underneath Robert's sail.

"Keep clear!" Ben yelled. "Rule Eleven—keep clear!" And now it was Robert who had to angle off *his* course as their boats plunged and bucked toward the starting line, side by side.

The timer on Ben's wrist beeped just as the air horn wailed—*Rheeeeehp!*—and they both squeaked past the buoy, two fair starts, with Robert barely a half length ahead. A blast of spray from the other boat's bow hit Ben in the face, but he shook it off with a grin. This was a *race*!

His hands were already stiff and cramped from the cold, and he was glad this first run toward the northern marker was a simple reach. With the wind steady and mostly from behind, he felt it was safe to fasten the rope in a cleat so he could let go and flex his aching fingers. But moments later the wind began gusting, forcing him to make constant adjustments to keep the boat sailing at its best speed. When he wasn't leaning backward out over the water to keep the boat from heeling over too far, he used one hand to bail out another gallon or so of water, always trying to keep the tiller steady so the sail would stay at the perfect angle to the wind.

Even though Robert was doing all these same things, Ben still kept directly behind him as they neared the northern mark. He was already incredibly alert, but seeing that bobbing red buoy ahead sent a jolt of electricity through him. No cramped fingers, no frozen feet, no slashing spray, nothing mattered now except the tiller, the sail, the wind, and the boat, thumping and skittering ahead. Because this next turn was crucial.

Robert thought he was Super-Sailor, but out on the water Ben knew he had one weakness—he acted like the marker buoys were made of kryptonite. Robert had bumped into two marks early last season, and each time the penalty had cost him a victory. Ever since, he had been taking his marker turns extra wide, sometimes by as much as ten feet or more. And now SuperSailor was going to get a surprise.

As they came level with the red buoy, sure enough, Robert shot a good twelve feet past it before starting his turn. Ben gritted his teeth in concentration, and the moment the nose of his boat passed the buoy, he came about, swinging right around the buoy in one smooth motion. Now he was sailing south toward the next marker, and Robert was two full lengths behind him.

Ben grinned into the wind and wanted to yell something like, *Hey, Bigmouth, I thought you "owned" this course!* But that would have made *him* a bigmouth. So he just smiled and shivered and sailed for all he was worth. Because he knew Robert too well. The guy wasn't going to just lay in behind and follow him to the finish line. No, he was going to push himself and his brand-new boat and his Olympic racing sails to the limit, and take every risk he needed to in order to win. So Ben kept glancing back.

And sure enough, Robert had his sheet pulled in very tight and low, and was hanging so far back over the side of his boat that his head was almost brushing the waves. So Ben did the same, but it was tricky business. This northern part of the course was farther from shore, and there was a lot more wind out here, plus the gusts were stronger. One good microburst could smack the sail right into the water and flip the whole boat. But if Robert could manage it, then he could too.

The spray was thick and constant now, and the shallow foot well was filling up fast with water. Rats! Ben let the sail out a little and jammed the sheet into the cleat. The boat instantly slowed down. He grabbed the scoop, leaned forward, and began bailing like crazy. It was cold and risky work, and it was definitely going to cost him some time, but at eight pounds a gallon, water on board was no good. At least he knew that Robert would have to do the same thing at some point, so he could still keep his lead. If he was careful.

As he leaned forward to bail one last big scoop of water, a tremendous gust of wind hit the boat. Ben dropped the bailer, pulled the sheet loose, and tillered into the wind, all at the same time. Even so, his boat heeled so far over that a good ten gallons of seawater rushed in across his feet. But he kept his head, righted the boat, and began bailing again furiously to get his hull up out of the waves. He expected Robert to go flashing past him any second. But he didn't.

Ben glanced over his shoulder and . . . no sail. Thirty feet behind him he saw a white hull, its centerboard up in the air, completely capsized. Hah!

But thoughts of victory vanished instantly. He couldn't spot an orange life vest . . . He didn't see Robert.

Reversing course in a flash, Ben reached the turtled boat in fifteen seconds. He let go of his sheet, then yanked the mast ropes loose so his sail dropped to the deck.

"Robert!" he shouted. Nothing—except terrible possibilities. Ben looked around for help. The finish-line motorboat was speeding toward him, but it was still at least a minute away, much too long.

Ben kicked off his shoes, then ripped off his life vest. He took a deep breath and dove into the freezing water next to Robert's boat. It was like plunging into a silent slow-motion movie, and he saw Robert right away, arms and legs out like a snow angel. Unconscious! And trapped! The buoyant life vest held him pinned up against the hollow underside of the boat.

Even though his lungs were burning for a breath of air, Ben grabbed the front of Robert's vest with both hands. Using every last bit of strength, he pulled down hard, then quickly to the side. Once clear of the hull, Robert popped to the surface like a cork.

Back up in the noise of the wind and waves, Ben sucked in a gasp of air, and got some seawater, too. Coughing, he managed to flip Robert over so his face was above water. And that's when he saw the cut on Robert's forehead, just above one eye. He grabbed the collar of Robert's life jacket and used his other arm to pull toward his sailboat, which had drifted about fifteen feet away. But before he had taken three strokes, strong hands pulled Robert away from him, up and over the side of the motorboat.

And by the time Ben had been hoisted aboard, someone had already gotten the bulky vest off Robert and a woman was bending over him, starting CPR.

Clear the airway . . .

Robert's eyes were still shut, and his lips were blue. Someone put a blanket around Ben's shoulders, but he barely noticed.

. . . two short, gentle rescue breaths . . .

Ben had never seen a face so white. Except for the blood on Robert's forehead.

. . . and thirty shallow chest pumps, count them out.

Halfway through the chest pumps, Robert coughed. A flood of water gushed from his nose and mouth. He gasped, and the woman turned his head gently to the side to clear his airway, then gave him a couple smacks on the back. He retched more water onto the deck, plus a bunch of other stuff. And everyone aboard the boat cheered.

A minute later the motorboat was speeding toward the pier. Robert was bundled up in three wool blankets, stretched out on a cushioned bench. White tape and a piece of gauze covered his cut, and he was shaking all over, still deathly pale. The woman who had done the CPR held a plastic thermos for him, and he took a careful sip of something hot. And that's when he noticed Ben sitting about five feet away.

He looked confused. "Hey . . . I thought you were out ahead of me. What happened?"

Ben shrugged. "A lot of stuff."

Mr. Wirtz, the finish-line official, sat on the seat next to Ben. "I believe you two know each other already, but I think a fresh introduction is in order. Robert Gerritt, this is Benjamin Pratt, the young man who just saved your life."

There were two ambulances waiting at the pier, but Ben refused to get into the one for him. "I'm just wet. Really, I'm fine." And his parents agreed with Ben.

As two policemen kept the crowd of onlookers out of the way, the other paramedics hustled Robert into the second ambulance. Just before they closed the back doors, he lifted his head up off the stretcher and called out, "Hey, Pratt, I *know* I could have caught up to you. And I want a rematch, okay?"

Ben grinned at him. "Anytime."

A reporter from the *Edgeport Pennant* wanted Ben to describe the race and the rescue, but his mom shooed the young woman away. "No," she said firmly. "We've got to get him home now." And as she guided Ben by one elbow, his dad moved out ahead of them, opening a path through the crowd.

Once they got to the parking lot, his dad took Ben's other elbow. He didn't really need help, but he let his knees sag a little anyway. And both his parents held on tight. It felt good.

When they were almost to the car, his dad gave Ben's arm an extra squeeze. "You did great out there," he said, "in every way. We're so proud of you."

His mom nodded and smiled. "I know Robert has never been your favorite person in the world, but right now, I can guarantee that you're *his* favorite. And his parents', too."

Ben still had the blanket wrapped around him like a sleeping bag, so he had to back his way into the front seat of his mom's car and then swing his legs inside.

His dad buckled him in and then pushed his damp hair up off his forehead. "See you next Saturday, okay? And we'll talk this week. Really a great day, Ben, a great day. So, I'll see you."

"See you, Dad."

His father started to shut the car door, but suddenly pulled it wide again, then leaned in and kissed Ben on the top of his head. "I'm just so glad you're safe, Ben."

"Me too, Dad."

"Good. So, I'll see you."

Ben nodded and smiled up into his dad's face as he shut the door, then watched as he turned and began walking back toward Parson's Marina.

And right away Ben felt like he had to show his mom he wasn't having unhappy thoughts, even though he was. Because that always made her sad. And then it was harder for both of them.

So he turned to his mom and smiled. "What you said about Robert? It's true—I've never liked that guy. At all. But when his boat flipped, I just went on autopilot or something."

"Well, your father was right, you certainly did everything great out there, and we're very proud of you."

She started the car, but before she had put it in gear, there was a tap on Ben's window. He turned quickly, thinking it was his dad again.

But it was Jill, with a pair of binoculars hanging around her neck.

He smiled and put his window down.

"Hi, Ben. Hi, Mrs. Pratt."

"Hi, Jill," she said. "It's good to see you."

"Good to see you, too."

"What are you doing here?" Ben said.

"What do you think? I'm a *huge* sailing fan, so I came to watch the race. And instead I got to see the big rescue scene—very cool. Hero stuff."

"Nah," said Ben, "it just sort of . . . happened."

"Right. Well, anyway, just wanted to say hi. And I can't wait to talk to Robert, to hear his side of the story."

"Yeah," said Ben, "maybe *he's* the one who rescued *me*."

Jill smiled. "Anyway, see you Monday. And be sure to e-mail me the stuff about that social studies project, okay?"

"Right," he said. "See you Monday."

As his mom drove out of the parking lot, she said, "You two are working on a social studies project?"

"Yeah, just some stuff we're doing for extra credit. About the history of the Oakes School."

"Hmm," his mom said, "that sounds like fun."

"Yeah," said Ben. "I think it's going to be pretty interesting."

KEEP A LOOKOUT FOR BOOK 2 IN THE BENJAMIN PRATT & THE KEEPERS OF THE SCHOOL SERIES

Also by Andrew Clements

A Million Dots

Benjamin Pratt & the Keepers of the School
We the Children • *Fear Itself*

Big Al

Big Al and Shrimpy

Dogku

Extra Credit

Frindle

Jake Drake, Bully Buster

Jake Drake, Class Clown

Jake Drake, Know-It-All

Jake Drake, Teacher's Pet

The Jacket

The Janitor's Boy

The Landry News

The Last Holiday Concert

Lost and Found

Lunch Money

No Talking

The Report Card

Room One

The School Story

A Week in the Woods

A READING GROUP GUIDE TO
WE THE CHILDREN
BOOK 1 OF
BENJAMIN PRATT & THE
KEEPERS OF THE SCHOOL

BY ANDREW CLEMENTS

DISCUSSION QUESTIONS

1. One of the first things readers learn about Ben is that he has caps on his front teeth. What happened to his front teeth? How does this experience affect his feelings about saving Oakes School?

2. What does Mr. Keane give Ben? Who owned this object before Mr. Keane? Why does Mr. Keane believe the school is about to be attacked?

3. Who was Duncan Oakes? What objects in and around the school remind students of Captain Oakes? Does your school have paintings, statues, trophies, or other items that help students remember its past? Do you ever think about these items? If so, describe one or more of these items and what thoughts, ideas, or inspirations they bring to you.

4. In Chapter 3, Ben thinks, *Welcome to the exciting new theme of Benjamin Pratt's life—change*. List three changes about which Ben is thinking. How does Ben feel about all these changes? Is change a theme in your life? If so, in what ways?

5. Who is Mr. Lyman? Why is he different from past janitors at Oakes School? What secrets does Jill discover about Mr. Lyman? In addition to Mr. Lyman, from whom do Ben and Jill keep Mr. Keane's coin and last words secret? Do you think this is a good decision? Why or why not?

6. How does Ben feel about sailing an Optimist? How long has he been sailing? What other student at Oakes races sailboats? Are the attitudes of this student toward sailing and school the same as Ben's? Explain your answer.

7. How has his parents' separation affected Ben? Describe Ben's different relationships with his mom and his dad. What evidence in the story suggests that Ben is hoping his parents will get back together? What advice might you give Ben about his parents' separation?

8. Why do Ben and Jill want to save Oakes School? What arguments could be made for and against the new amusement park? How would you feel if a devel-

oper wanted to build a new amusement park in your town? How would you feel if your school was at risk of being demolished to make room for another type of new building?

9. How does Ben's sailing experience help him figure out the meaning of the mysterious instructions on the coin and how they relate to Oakes School? Where is the "rose" on the floor? To what do the rose and coin lead Ben and Jill?

10. What do Ben and Jill find inside the square of pine? What do you think the inscription means? Do you think Duncan Oakes's idea to entrust the school to the children was a good one? Why or why not?

11. On the morning of the race, how does Ben prepare himself and his Optimist? What observations does he make about the race spectators, including his mom and dad? What does Ben love about sailing? Do you participate in a sport or other activity that makes you feel similar to the way Ben feels when he is out on the water? Does this feeling help you in other aspects of your life? If so, in what way?

12. On the last page of the book, Ben and Jill discuss Ben's rescue of Robert. Ben tells them, "maybe *he's* the one who rescued *me*." Did Ben need rescuing?

What do you think Ben learned about himself from the experience of saving Robert? How do you think the rescue experience has affected his feelings about being a Keeper of the School?

WRITING AND RESEARCH ACTIVITIES

I. *WE THE CHILDREN*

1. Readers are drawn right into history with the book title, *We the Children*, a twist on the first words of the preamble to America's Constitution. Go to the library or online to learn more about the Constitution, the people who wrote it, and the reason the document was created. Then write a paragraph explaining why you think Andrew Clements chose to name his story this way.

2. Like the writers of the Constitution, Duncan Oakes and his community could not have foreseen exactly what would happen to his school and town in the future. With friends or classmates, make a list of at least twenty changes to life in America that Duncan Oakes probably could not have imagined, such as things like cell phones and places like Disney World. Take a class vote to see which change

people think would have surprised Duncan Oakes most of all.

3. How do you think not knowing what the future would hold affected what was written on the copper tablet found by Ben and Jill? In the character of a present-day historian examining the copper tablet, write a one- to three-paragraphs long report explaining why you think the message on the tablet was written in such a mysterious way.

4. Write a one-page letter to students one hundred years in the future. Think of an important message you would like to share or an important object you would like future schoolchildren of the future to notice. As you write, make sure to consider what the recipients of your letter might be able to understand about the technology and history of the twenty-first century. What might be a good place to store your letter?

5. Interview a grandparent or other older adult about what life was like when he or she was your age. Here are some possible questions: What was life like without cell phones, handheld music devices, or the Internet? What was television like? How did he or she get news and information? How did one make plans with friends? What was school like? What did

kids do after school? What was the city or town like? Does he or she think life is better or worse for kids today than it was when he or she was young? Prepare a short oral report to share information from your interview with friends or classmates, or collect all of the interviews from friends and classmates into an oral history notebook to keep in your school library.

II. BUILT INTO HISTORY

1. Much about American history can be learned from its buildings and architecture. Go to the library or online to learn more about historic buildings in America. Start by visiting the U.S. General Services Administration's website (www.gsa.gov/portal/content/102069) or the Library of Congress's Historic American Buildings Survey and Historic American Engineering Record Collections (memory.loc.gov/ammem/collections/habs_haer/hhmap.html). Make a list of five buildings you would like to visit and why. Or write a short speech or newspaper-style article explaining why you feel it is important (or not important) to preserve historic buildings. Use examples from your research and quotes from *We the Children* to support your argument.

2. Ben lives in a coastal New England town, full of maritime history. Visit Smith's Master Index to Maritime Museums (www.maritimemusuems.net) and find a museum of interest to you. Plan a trip to visit this museum. How would you get there? Where would you stay? Where would you eat? What museum exhibits will you visit? Are there other historic sites near the museum you will also visit? Write up your itinerary to share with friends, family members, or classmates.

3. In what year was your school built and what grades were taught at that time? What was the population of your town in the year your school was built? What changes have been made to the school building or its purpose? Has your town or city population changed? In what important ways is your town now different from the way it was when your school was new? Compile your answers to these questions, and others of your choice, into an informational booklet about your school and its place in the community.

4. On a large sheet of poster board, create a sign headlined WELCOME TO OAKES SCHOOL. Based on details from the novel, complete the poster with an illustrated list of highlights, points of interest, and other

details you might post at the entrance to a historical school building.

5. Make a top-ten list of reasons to save Oakes School, and another list of reasons to allow the theme park to be built. Divide your class into two groups, to debate for and against the demolition of Oakes School to build an amusement park.

III. KEEPERS OF THE SCHOOL

1. Before he dies, Mr. Keane tells Ben how the coin was passed down from previous janitors dating back to the time of Duncan Oakes. In the character of Mr. Keane, or another past janitor, write a journal entry describing what happened on the day you were given the coin and how you felt about your new responsibility.

2. Imagine you are Thomas Vining, Louis Hendley, or Abigail Baynes, one of the three children who signed the sheet of copper found by Ben and Jill. In the character of one of these children, write a journal entry describing how you felt about putting your name to this document and why you feel this might be important in terms of your hopes and dreams for the future of yourself and your town.

3. You are a student at Oakes School. Ben and Jill have told you about the coin and the discoveries they have made and have asked you to help them with their mission to save the school. Write an outline describing the plan you would suggest that they follow.

4. In the character of Ben or Jill, write a poem or song lyrics encouraging your classmates to help save Oakes School. Begin with the words, "We the children."

5. Imagine *We the Children* is being made into a movie! Draw the movie poster featuring Ben and Jill fighting to save Oakes School. Include an exciting sentence or two to encourage school kids to watch the film.

This guide was prepared by Stasia Ward Kehoe, a freelance writer and author specializing in the interests of young readers. She holds a master's degree in Performance Studies from New York University, and teaches writing and theater to elementary school students in western Washington.

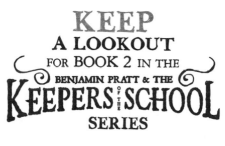

FEAR ITSELF

Hero to Zero

Benjamin Pratt had some serious detective work to do, so his plan was to be invisible all day, to do nothing that would draw attention to himself. He was going to glide around the Captain Oakes School like a ghost, observing, examining, analyzing. He had a fresh pack of index cards for organizing his notes, and he'd brought his good digital camera, a tiny thing not much bigger than a pack of gum. He also had a small flashlight and a twelve-foot tape measure. Secret agent stuff.

But the invisibility wasn't happening, not today.

"Ben, way to go!"

"Hey, Pratt—saving Gerritt and everything? Amazing!"

Before he got to his homeroom on Monday he'd been high-fived four times, and had been called a hero, the champ, Mr. Lifeguard, and Aquaman.

True, he had in fact dived into the choppy ocean to help Robert Gerritt after the guy flipped his sailboat during their race on Saturday. But only because he'd been right there when it happened—what, was he supposed to just watch a kid drown?

When a crowd of reporters had gathered at his mom's house Saturday evening with lights and cameras, she had scolded them off her lawn. Ben didn't have anything more to say about it—another boy had been in trouble, and her son had helped out, that was all.

But Robert had had plenty to say.

Propped up in a hospital bed with a bandage wrapping his head, he had talked to everybody. The incident was called "Rescue at Sea" on one Boston TV station and "Escape from Death" on another—a colorful news story both Saturday and Sunday.

To Ben's surprise, Robert had actually given him some credit.

Looking straight into the camera, he'd said, "Yeah, if it hadn't been for Ben, I might not have made it."

However, Robert had also said, "But the worst part? It happened just as I was about to win my first big sailing race of the year!"

Typical.

And today, with everyone treating Ben like a celebrity, he didn't see how he'd get to do much

exploring. Which was too bad—he really needed some fresh ideas.

All weekend he had been chewing on the clues he and Jill had found on Friday, clues that were supposed to help them find stuff—stuff that would somehow keep their school from being torn down . . . that would somehow keep the Glennley Entertainment Group from building their massive theme park on the harbor . . . that would somehow keep the whole town of Edgeport from turning into a huge, neon tourist trap.

That was the mission, and it seemed impossible. Plus completely crazy.

After the final bell clanged for homeroom,

everyone stood up and recited the Pledge of Alle giance, and then the principal began reading the announcements. But Ben couldn't think about anything except those clues. They ran through his mind for the hundredth time:

After five bells sound, time to sit down.
After four times four, tread up one more.
After three hooks pass, one will be brass.
After two tides spin, a man walks in.
After one still star, horizons afar.

He had called Jill twice on Sunday and again this morning before school to ask if she'd made any progress.

"Give it a rest, Benjamin. I *know* we need a breakthrough—but, like, what are we looking for? And where are we supposed to start? And what could we possibly find that could actually stop these people? The Glennley Group has spent *thirty-five million dollars*. They *own* the school. And on June eighteenth, they're going to rip it down. I've got to eat breakfast. Good-bye."

She'd sounded angry, discouraged, too, which wasn't like her. Ben couldn't figure it out. Jill had been rock solid last Friday, and she'd seemed great when he'd seen her after the sailboat race on Saturday. So . . . something must have happened over the rest of the weekend. But what? He had no idea. Whatever was bothering her, it wasn't good. Because Ben was pretty sure that without Jill's help on this, they might as well go ahead and buy the cheap lifetime passes that Tall Ships Ahoy! had advertised in Sunday's *Boston Globe*.

But he'd see Jill in third-period math for sure, and maybe he'd have something figured out by then. Or at least have an idea about what to do next. Maybe she just needed to feel like they were making some real progress. Ben was ready to try anything to cheer her up a little.

Ms. Wilton took attendance, then laid out the week's schedule. When she finished, there were still about ten minutes before first period. So Ben got out a pencil and a blank index card and started thinking.

He thought about the copper plate he and Jill had found in a secret compartment on the third floor—a message hidden there by the first Keepers of the School back in 1791. One particular sentence about Captain Oakes in that message jumped out at him: *He prepared five safeguards to help us in our self-defense.*

Ben wrote the word "safeguards" on the card.

Maybe Jill was right. Maybe Captain Oakes was

just a rich old weirdo who wanted lots of attention, the kind of guy who would stick his own grave in the middle of a school playground.

No, Ben was already sure there was something more to all this.

He thought about the message stamped on the gold coin Mr. Keane had given him, and then wrote two more words on the index card: "attack" and "defend."

Those were military terms.

Which made sense—after all, Captain Oakes was a *captain*, a man of action, the guy in charge. He had commanded one of his own ships in the American navy during the Revolutionary War.

Ben stared at the three words he'd written and tried to imagine being a sea captain, being responsible for a large ship and the life of every person on it. The captain would have to oversee everything. His ship would sail thousands of miles, spend months at a time on the high seas. The captain would have to account for every barrel of water, every sack of flour, every yard of canvas, every musket and cannonball, every ounce of gunpowder, every length of rope.

So Captain Oakes wasn't some goofball. He must

have been an amazing thinker, an incredible long-range planner.

And . . . as the captain was converting his warehouse into this school, it was like he was outfitting a ship for a trip—the long voyage into the future. And he was certain there would be dangers.

Ben remembered the old book the librarian had found for him, and what he'd read about the captain. Oakes had been very old by then, so he knew he wouldn't be around to command this new ship himself. If it ever came under attack, his officers would have to fight the enemy on their own. *But* . . . if he planned carefully and left the right kind of weapons—safeguards—then his ship and his crew would survive.

And who did the captain enlist as the commanders for his most important ship? The school janitors.

Ben smiled. That was pure genius, to choose steady, professional caretakers to defend his school, to carry that gold coin with their captain's instructions on it. And down through the years, each janitor had been responsible for finding his own replacement, someone trustworthy.

And the captain's plan had worked perfectly from 1783 right up to last Thursday. Except now, there wasn't a reliable janitor. Which was why Mr. Keane had given the coin to Ben.

So *I'm* the new commander, he thought, and his smile got bigger.

But it faded as he thought about Mr. Keane. Just hours after handing the coin to Ben, he had died.

And he had warned Ben about his assistant janitor, Lyman: "He's a snake."

Worse than a snake, thought Ben.

He was a spy, working for the company that had bought the school—after they'd figured out how to get around the captain's last will and testament.

Lyman was a big problem.

"Ben?"

He looked up to see his homeroom teacher holding out her hand, and he took a slip of paper from her.

"I almost forgot. Mrs. Sinclair wants to see you in the library before first period."

"Oh—okay."

He tucked the index card in his pocket and stood up.

"And Ben, I heard about what you did this weekend. I'm proud of you."

"Thanks," he said, beginning to blush, "but really, I was just the closest one to the accident."

"Well," Ms. Wilton said, "I'm proud of you anyway—we all are," and there were nods of agreement from the kids around him.

Ben smiled awkwardly, his face bright red now. He grabbed his book bag and rushed out the door.

So much for being invisible.

The library was on the opposite corner of the first floor, and as he walked through the quiet hallway, Ben knew why Mrs. Sinclair wanted to see him. He and Jill were doing a big social studies project, a report about the history of the Oakes School—which would give them extra time in the building to search for the stuff the captain had left behind, the safeguards.

A brilliant plan—*his* brilliant plan.

Except Robert Gerritt had butted his way into the project. So that would be a drag. And a complication—one more among a jillion others.

Ben shook his head. This whole thing was crazy. In less than a month the school was scheduled for demolition, and two kids were supposed to stop it all by themselves? But Ben caught himself, made himself stop thinking that way—he was sounding like Jill! And if they *both* got discouraged, that really would be the end. He had to keep fighting. Still . . . it all seemed pretty insane.

When he walked in from the hallway, Mrs. Sinclair saw him. She nodded toward the glass-walled workroom over in the center of the library. "I'll be with you in a minute, Ben."

The library was his favorite place in the old school, so he was glad to have a moment to just sit and look around. It was a large space, and the high ceiling made it feel open and airy. Dark oak bookshelves ran along all four walls of the main room. The shelf edges had been carved to look like thick rope, and the panels along the top of each unit had also been decorated. Some of the carvings showed scenes of ships at sea, complete with waves and clouds and flapping flags. There were carvings of small New England farms and busy seaports, and Ben's favorite showed a large deer standing on a wooded hillside. The designer of the room had added three shallow alcoves, which broke up the boxy feeling of the long shelves. Centered on the north, east, and west walls, each alcove had a dark oak table and comfy cushioned benches. Wide leaded-glass windows facing east and north let in lots of daylight. Even though the center area had been updated with modern tables and chairs and computer workstations, the original flavor of the room had survived. The place smelled like time.

Looking around, Ben's thoughts drifted again to Captain Oakes and the safeguards he and Jill had to find. He was glad the library was going to be sort of like the command center for their project, a place they could come before and after school. And since he and Jill would need to make lots of drawings and take lots of photos for the report, they would be able to wander around the school pretty much wherever they wanted to. At least, that was the plan.

His brilliant plan.

Mrs. Sinclair came into the workroom and stood in front of him. He looked up with a smile—which disappeared when he saw her face.

"The book is missing, Ben, the one you used on Friday." Her voice was flat and cold. "I took it off the reference shelf for you, and you promised to be careful with it. But this morning, Ms. Shubert noticed it wasn't there."

Ben felt his throat tighten, felt his face start to get hot. "But I—"

She held up a hand. "No, let me finish. I haven't talked about this with Mr. Telmer, or with anyone else. I wanted to speak to you first. If for some reason you misunderstood me, and you took that book out of the library, then you can simply return it. And as long as it isn't damaged, that will be the end of this. All right?" She looked him in the eye. "Now, what do you have to say?"

GREAT MIDDLE-GRADE FICTION FROM
Andrew Clements,
MASTER OF THE SCHOOL STORY

FRINDLE

THE SCHOOL STORY

NO TALKING

THE LANDRY NEWS

ROOM ONE

LOST AND FOUND

THE JANITOR'S BOY

A WEEK IN THE WOODS

EXTRA CREDIT

"Few contemporary writers portray the public school world better than Clements."—*New York Times Book Review*

From Atheneum Books for Young Readers
Published by Simon & Schuster
KIDS.SimonandSchuster.com